PLAYED IN SEATTLE

A JULIA FAIRCHILD MYSTERY

PJ PETERSON

FINNGIRL, LLC

CHAPTER

ONE

Traces of snow on the highest peaks of the Olympic Mountains stood out against brilliant blue skies as Julia and Carly traveled north on Interstate 5 to Seattle.

Julia and Carly had just passed the multiple entrances to JBLM, officially known as Joint Base Lewis-McChord, which was the home of the United States Army I Corps and the 62nd Airlift Wing. The traffic along this part of I-5 between Olympia and Tacoma was brutal during weekdays when the commuters added their numbers to the thousands of military and civilian personnel who worked at the base itself. On this beautiful Saturday in May, Julia was able to cruise along at a comfortable seventy miles per hour, and had thus far not encountered any delays due to accidents or other mishaps.

"We should be pulling up at the hotel shortly after two o'clock," said Julia.

"I don't understand why you decided to visit Seattle for a whole week," said Carly. "It's not like you've never been here."

"Like I told you last week, Josh and I had planned to do all

1

the things normal tourists do when they come here for the first time. Even though he's not coming, after all, I decided to take the week off anyway and play tourist. When I was getting my bachelor's degree here at the U of Washington, I didn't have the time or the money to do half the things you and I are going to do." She smiled at her sister.

"I've been hesitant to ask about Josh," said Carly, giving Julia a little sideways look. "Is there something you want to tell me?"

Julia sighed wistfully. "His company decided to open an office in New York City instead of on the west coast. Josh was asked to be in charge of setting it up, and he couldn't turn it down. He's entrenched on the east coast and loves what he does there as much as I'm happy to stay on this side of the country." She sighed again. "It's so difficult to have a serious relationship from 2,500 miles away, so we agreed to call it a day. Maybe I'll be sorry in the future, but his heart is some-where else right now. And I really don't want to move to New York and start all over with a new medical practice."

"I get it. And I'm so sorry it worked out like that." Carly patted her sister's arm. "Someday, you'll meet the right guy. Be patient."

"The perennial optimist," replied Julia. "But thanks for the encouragement. And thank you for joining me. It's always more fun to share experiences with someone."

"As long as you feed me and let me have cookies now and then, I think it'll be great," said Carly. "And no dead bodies."

Julia laughed. "I promise."

"I've heard that before, sis."

Julia could only shrug. Carly was right: she'd been with her sister previously, and either from being in the wrong place at the wrong time or needing to help with her medical expertise, they had, in fact, ended up with a dead body to deal with. But this was going to be a whole week to just have fun and explore the Emerald City.

∼

THE SISTERS LEANED on the rail of their balcony overlooking Elliot Bay and watched the harbor traffic. The mid-May day was sunny and full of promise for decent weather for the "Spooked in Seattle" tour Julia had reserved for their Saturday evening. They watched the ships and boats and ferries in silence for another while.

"That's the third cruise ship I've seen heading out of the harbor," said Carly. "I didn't realize there were so many options from Seattle. Are they all going to Alaska?"

"When I stayed here for a conference last fall, one of the desk clerks told me that two or three cruises leave from the docks from downtown and Elliott Bay almost daily. They may be going to Hawaii, or to Asia, or down the coast toward California or Mexico, in addition to the Inland Passage to Alaska. "

"So it's not just a Saturday departure anymore, as it was when Dad and I rode one of the cruise ships to Alaska," said Carly. "Of course, that was a few years ago now."

"He loved that trip. Cheers to Dad!" Julia and Carly smiled at each other. Their father had been a wonderful man, and they both missed him.

Julia Fairchild, M.D. and her younger sister Carly Pedersen had grown up with their four sibs on a small farm in southwest Washington state, four miles from the nearest town, as had their dad. Julia had always wanted to be a doctor and "help people" and had been practicing internal medicine for nearly ten years in Parkview. Though she'd planned to live and work any place other than where she'd been born, she was glad now that it had worked out that way.

Her workaholic nature made it a challenge to take time away from work, so she was determined to make the most of the week, despite her disappointment in breaking up with Josh. She was still single in her mid-thirties, although she had briefly been married right out of college. She wasn't unhappy or really lonely, she reminded herself. After all, she had a rewarding career and a great dog, Trixie, a rescue beagle mix, as her companion. Trixie seemed to enjoy her own vacations at a dear friend's kennel, where she became part of the household with the other resident dogs.

Carly, the youngest of the clan and four years younger than Julia, had finished college before returning to live on ten acres of their father's parents' homestead while also working in Parkview. She was married to a local guy, Rob, who congenially went along with his wife's need for "girl time" with her sister Julia. She had inherited the golden blonde curls of their mom, along with hazel eyes and an electric smile, while Julia, at two inches taller, resembled their dad, with her brunette bob and blue eyes. Although different in appearance, the sisters were similar in interests, as well as fast friends. One thing they both enjoyed was a spooky mystery.

"What is this tour you've lined up for tonight? I've never heard of it," said Carly.

"One of my friends told me about "Spooked in Seattle." She said it was spookier than all get-out."

"So, it's not the same as the "Underground Seattle" tour?"

"No, although there apparently is some crossover, from what I've read. I've done the other tour several times, but not in at least ten years. This one sounded like it was worth trying."

"With your luck, we'll probably see a real ghost," said Carly.

"At least a ghost would be dead already." Julia grinned at her sister.

~

THAT NIGHT, the pair of tour leaders told numerous stories of paranormal experiences that couldn't be explained in any rational manner. Julia's skin prickled as she listened to the believable tales that had been reported by multiple observers. She recalled that one of her neighbors told her of seeing the upstairs curtains being moved aside in her own home at a time when it was totally vacant. For that very reason, she always turned the lights on when she went upstairs, just in case Mrs. Weedman was still hanging about doing ghostly things. Since older homes had their share of creaks and squeaks, she wasn't convinced those in her own home were caused by real ghosts. But turning the light on couldn't hurt.

She had to chuckle when she thought of her neighbor using sage to rid her bedroom of the ghosts of its previous owners. Hayley, the dog, had started growling at one corner every night, so she went to a local mystic's shop and learned about the sage-burning method. It seemed to work, and the ghostly inhabitants moved out. Or, at least, her dog quit barking at the corner. She and Carly had also encountered the local spirit woman on Virgin Gorda using sage the previous fall. She had been burning the herb to exorcise the bad spirits from the area of the beach where the sisters had found a young woman dead a day or so earlier.

Julia and Carly sipped their glasses of Cabernet Sauvignon as they sat in the lounge after the final stop on the tour. A dozen or so of the other tour guests joined them in the darkened room.

"My skin is crawling," said Carly. "I'm not sure I want to go back outside after this tour."

"It was scary, to be sure," said Julia. "I've never experienced paranormal activity myself, or I don't think I have. Now I wonder."

"Let's get out of here and grab a taxi," said Carly. "It's almost the witching hour. And I want to be at the hotel before midnight."

Several small groups stood in front of the pub while waiting for a cab to pull up. Julia observed a quartet of men who emerged from an adjacent alley. One of them turned toward her and locked eyes. His eyes were wide and his face pale in the streetlight, as if he were terrorized, she thought.

"That man looks like he's seen a ghost," she said, pointing a finger in his direction. "I've never seen such a frightened look. Do you remember seeing him on the tour?"

The man had turned his face away and was being helped into a taxi by the time Carly spotted him. "I'm not sure. All I saw was the side of this face."

CHAPTER

TWO

"I haven't been in a canoe in years," said Julia. "Do you want the front or the back?"

"I can't remember which one is better for novices, so let's go by alphabetical order. I'll take the front end."

The sisters managed to get into the canoe without tipping it over and successfully maneuvered the skinny boat from the canoe house at the University of Washington into Union Bay. They gained confidence as they continued to move along the shoreline and across the Montlake Cut to the arboretum.

"Wow," said Carly as they cruised under the freeway that went east across Lake Washington toward Bellevue, "it's amazingly quiet on the water, even under the freeway."

"That's what I love about being on the water. The sound above us is much less than when we're level with it."

The oars made soft swish sounds as they paddled around the quiet water of the arboretum in the late afternoon. They had slept in this morning after their spooky tour before heading for a day of relaxing in the outdoors. The spring flowers were in full bloom, with rhododendrons and azaleas in various stages of opening their blossoms.

"I didn't know there were so many varieties of Japanese maples," said Carly. "I bet I've seen at least thirty different leaf types already."

"This is heaven," said Julia. "I haven't done this in at least fifteen years—not since I was a student at the U."

"I'm glad you suggested this. I was apprehensive about getting into a canoe with you, but this was worth it." Carly pretended to duck in case Julia splashed water at her.

"Are you ready to head back?"

"Yeah, I guess so. My arms are getting tired."

"Same here," said Julia. "Let's see what's around this next corner and call it good."

The canoe glided through the water into a long, shallow indentation along the bank. Julia and Carly prepared to make a 180-degree turn toward the boathouse, with Julia doing the steering from the rear.

"Julia, look to your right. I see something along the bank. Is that what I think it is?"

Julia looked in the direction that Carly was pointing. "Let's get closer. I'm not sure what we're seeing, but I'm afraid it's a body."

Carly groaned as they approached the partially-submerged body, now clearly visible on the bank. "Oh! I think I saw an arm move. Hurry, Julia!"

Julia clambered out of the boat and rushed to the body while Carly secured the canoe. She quickly checked his carotid artery for a pulse, though she was afraid the man was dead. The man was lying face down on the shallow bank, his arms sprawled out, his left hand in the water. He had an obvious head injury and was oozing blood from an open wound on the crown of his head. She felt a faint, thready pulse and yelled to

Carly, "Call 911! He's alive." She turned him over after assuring herself that he didn't have an obvious neck injury, and covered him with her jacket to help keep him warm in the waning afternoon sun.

"Sir, can you hear me?" Julia asked him. He appeared to be sleeping, but Julia knew better. When she opened his eyes to check his pupils, she did a double take. She thought she recognized his face. She checked his respiration and, although his breaths were shallow, he didn't seem in immediate danger.

"Emergency people are on the way," said Carly. "I'm going to wait at the edge of the parking lot and lead them here."

"Wait a sec. They won't be here for a couple of minutes, so will you take a closer look at him? Isn't this the man who turned to look at us last night after the ghost tour?"

Carly moved in closer, looked at the man's face and gasped. "I think you're right, although I didn't see him straight on then, but these look like the clothes he was wearing. I wonder what happened."

"I wish I knew. I'm going to take a picture in case he's already gone when the police get here." Julia took a quick photo of his face, then searched quickly for anything to help answer that question. She wouldn't do anything to contaminate the crime scene or rifle through his pockets at the risk of being yelled at by the police once they arrived. But she noticed a bit of paper peeking out from under the man's hand that was stretched out on the dirt. Carly started to leave but turned back to Julia when her sister said, "Carly. This might be something." With her shirt sleeve pulled down over her own hand, she lifted his hand a wee bit to see what was under it. It was a rumpled scrap of paper that appeared to have been torn from a playbill or a notice of some kind, such as is often found posted on a kiosk.

Julia snapped a picture of the paper scrap and carefully replaced the hand.

"What does it say?" Carly asked, mollified by Julia's taking proper care of potential clues.

"I can only read a few words, but 'nuclear' is one of them. Someone added a penciled note that said 'Space Center,' but that's all I could decipher." She shook her head, puzzled.

"Hmm. How does this guy go from being downtown at midnight to the arboretum the next morning? And what does the Space Center have to do with any of this? And why did *we* have to find him?" Carly sighed. "I'd better go to the parking lot. I hear sirens coming this way."

THE EMERGENCY CREW arrived a few moments later, with Carly leading the way. Seattle's emergency services had been well known for rapid response since the early days of Medic One. The EMTs quickly executed an overall assessment, started intravenous fluids, and whisked the still-unconscious man onto a gurney for transport to University Hospital, which was nearest, just across the Montlake bridge.

A police car siren announced its arrival on the scene a moment before the ambulance closed its doors. The lead EMT confirmed to the police that the man was alive but was seriously injured. He gave the detective a minute to check the man's pockets for any personal effects before he left for the emergency department, sirens blaring.

Julia gave the detective a couple of minutes to assess the scene before she approached him. He was going to want to know why she and Carly were in the area, anyway.

He seemed satisfied with his search and waved Julia and

Carly over. "I'm Detective Danny Monroe. I'm assuming that you called 911."

Julia said, "Yes, Sir. I'm Dr. Julia Fairchild. This is my sister Carly. She called while I stayed with him until the ambulance arrived." Julia gave him an abbreviated version of finding him facedown on the bank when they were canoeing, and that they recognized him from last night.

Detective Monroe seemed very interested in Julia's observation that the John Doe on the bank in front of them had appeared to be frightened when they saw him the previous evening. Julia described the look on his face as one of sheer terror. "I thought he looked like he'd seen a ghost. Now I wonder if he was trying to tell us he needed help."

Julia and Carly described the other men as best they could from having seen them on the tour as well as outside. They were all dark-haired, were attired in casual clothing, and had on dark-tinted glasses, despite the evening hour.

Detective Monroe had searched the man's pockets and found them empty. Julia confirmed they hadn't searched the man's pockets before the police or EMT personnel arrived.

Monroe asked if Julia and Carly had heard him talk the evening before.

"Hmm, no, not a word, now that you mention it," said Julia. "I just saw his face when he turned toward me. He didn't say anything. He just looked straight into my eyes. I wish I had done something, but it all happened so quickly."

"I'm not sure what you could have done," said Monroe. "We'll have a go at this the usual way and see if his fingerprints or face show up in any of our databases. You two are free to go. Thank you for your help."

"Maybe that scrap of paper he was holding might be helpful," Julia offered.

"Scrap of paper?" Monroe frowned.

"Yes, didn't you see it? It was in his hand."

"He wasn't holding anything. I checked him out before the medics took him."

Julia looked for the scrap of paper that she had seen under the man's hand, but it wasn't anywhere to be found. She described it to the detective, who promised to check with the EMTs when he interviewed them at the hospital.

"I have a picture of it if that would help," said Julia.

Monroe looked at her with a furrowed brow, then at the picture. "You say this gentleman was holding this piece of paper? Maybe it had been laying there in the grass already, and he grasped it when he struggled after he was on the ground."

Julia shrugged. "Maybe. I could only read a few words, but 'nuclear' is one of them." She pointed at the photograph. "Someone added a penciled note that read 'Space Center,' but that's all I could decipher." She shook her head, puzzled. "Do you want me to send this to your email? I have a photo of his face, too, if that would help."

"Sure, send them both. We can start doing facial identity checks right away. Here's my card with everything you need to know to contact me."

"Will you check the security footage around that taxi stand? Maybe you'll find video footage of the men."

"That's standard practice, Miss Fairchild," he replied with a dark look.

Julia pulled a business card from her wallet and handed it to the detective. "We'll be in town all week if you think we can help."

Once the detective had walked back to his car, Julia took one last look around before she and Carly readied the canoe for the trip back.

They had less physical and emotional energy on the return

trip to the canoe house, and had to fight a headwind and whitecaps, as well.

"I forgot that the wind usually picks up as the day goes on and is usually going the wrong direction when you're tired and in a canoe," said Julia.

They paddled along quietly against the wind for the next ten minutes before Julia spoke again. "I wonder how that guy ended up at the arboretum."

"No detective work. You promised. Or I'll make you do all the paddling the rest of the way back."

CHAPTER

THREE

Just like the lyric from an old song about the "bluest sky you'll ever see," the sun shone brightly on a brilliant May Monday. "This is a perfect day to go to the Seattle Center and have lunch in the restaurant at the top of the Space Needle," said Julia.

"Wouldn't we need reservations?" asked Carly.

Julia smiled and held up a piece of paper with the confirmation for lunch for two people at eleven thirty. "Josh was going to treat me, but now I'll treat you instead."

"I don't think I've ever been to the top," said Carly.

"I've taken the elevator up to the observation level but haven't eaten in the restaurant itself because of the prices. Mom raised us to be too frugal, I'm afraid. But today is worth celebrating."

"Are we celebrating something I don't know about?" asked Carly, now a little wary.

Julia laughed. "No, silly. I've been doing some mindfulness reading lately, and finding something to celebrate every day is part of my new mantra."

"Hm. So how do you celebrate a day when you find someone near death at the arboretum?"

"Well, I can be thankful for emergency personnel and excellent hospitals."

"That seems like hedging, but I get what you mean," said Carly. "I'll be thankful that guy wasn't dead, and you don't have to get dragged into another murder case."

"That, too."

THE TEN-BLOCK WALK to the Seattle Center was noisy because of the Monday traffic on the city streets. "I'm glad we decided to walk," said Julia. "Parking is horrendous here almost any day, on top of the heavy traffic getting here. I'm convinced we'll get there faster on foot than with our car today. The GPS said it's seventeen minutes from the hotel."

"Yeah. I'm just glad *you're* driving around here. I've not ever lived in a big city as you have. We don't even have a traffic light in our little hometown."

"True. If we're too tired after lunch and touring the Science Center, we can take an Uber back. In fact, we have a few minutes to look around now if you want. I hate to waste this beautiful weather waiting in a lobby for our table."

"What's going on at the Pacific Science Center? I thought it was exhibits for kids."

"Originally, during the World's Fair in 1962, that was mostly true. Since then, according to its website, it's evolved into many kinds of exhibits and activities. What I'm interested in is the Laser Dome."

"What's so cool about that?"

"One of my friends said her son works there. I looked up some of their videos on YouTube and was really impressed. I can't imagine what it's like to see those fantastic light shows in real life. Better than fireworks, I'll bet."

Julia wandered to a kiosk in front of the Science Center, hoping to find a schedule of other activities. She squealed. "Carly, come here. Look at this."

Carly followed Julia's finger and read the short article about a nuclear symposium that was being held. "Yeah. So?"

Julia found the photo she'd taken of the scrap of paper the day before. "Look at this. I think it was torn from a flyer for this symposium."

Carly peered at the image and at the flyer in front of her. "They sure look like they could be a match. So what? We're not playing detective, remember?"

Julia put her hands up. "I know. I find it curious. That's all. But I'd kinda like to poke my head into the auditorium for a minute after lunch."

Carly exhaled loudly. "Well, I suppose that couldn't hurt."

"Let's go on up to the restaurant. The Space Needle is off to our left."

When they turned around and walked two hundred feet, they were squarely at the base of the huge tower.

"Wow!" said Carly. "The Space Needle looks huge when we're this close to it." She tilted her head back and forth. "It doesn't really look like a needle, does it? More like a spaceship on top of a skinny rocket."

Julia and Carly gazed out the window as the restaurant slowly turned, mesmerizing them with a full 360-degree view of the cityscape during a one-hour revolution. Carly said, "That was an amazing lunch. I'm sure I've never eaten better Chicken

Marsala. And why is a fresh green salad in a restaurant better than what we create at home?"

Julia laughed. "Even though I was named the 'Betty Crocker Homemaker of Tomorrow' in my high school home economics class, I'm sure I can't tell you. They do seem to have a secret, though, don't they?"

"How was that salmon? I eat fish all the time at home with Rob bringing it home from the river so I wasn't tempted. But it looked tasty."

"Yum." Julia licked her lips. "It was grilled on a cedar plank and had just the right touch of honey, ginger and lemon. I think I detected some soy in the sauce as well. As you said, we can try making it at home, but it's hard to duplicate these recipes in our own humble kitchens."

"Let's finish our wine and walk around the walkway outside the restaurant before we go down to that symposium," said Carly.

Julia pointed out some of her favorite Seattle landmarks from when she lived in Seattle during her university years. She told a tale of drinking her first beer at a beach party in Golden Gardens when she was still underage. "I couldn't figure out why everyone was so excited about drinking warm beer. Now I know I was supposed to drink it faster. It had been cold when I started."

"I'm surprised at the number of sailboats out on both Lake Union and Elliot Bay, considering it's a Monday," said Carly.

"They might be the retired folks who have the freedom of weekday sailing, or have a work schedule that gives them weekdays off," said Julia. "I read somewhere that Seattle has more boats than any other port on the west coast, including Los Angeles and San Diego."

"That's an interesting statistic. Bragging rights, I guess."

Julia checked her watch and said, "The symposium is starting in about fifteen minutes. We have just enough time to walk back over to the Pacific Science Center and find the auditorium."

"I can hardly wait," said Carly, discreetly rolling her eyes.

FOUR

Several dozen people, mostly men wearing khakis and shirts without ties, milled about in the hallway outside the entrance to the conference room where the conference was to be held. The poster outside the room read, "Nuclear Energy is Clean Energy." The symposium was sponsored by several agencies whose names were listed at the bottom.

"I thought nuclear energy was on the way out," said Carly. "What's all this about?"

"I was reading about it last night after I finished my novel. I wish I could write like Louise Penny." She sighed. "Anyway, I read that proponents tout all the benefits of nuclear energy being clean as opposed to fossil fuels. And relatively inexpensive. And useful."

"Yeah, and scary when nuclear plants blow up or leak radioactive material," Carly countered.

"Maybe, but nuclear energy is very valuable and efficient when used in other ways, such as in nuclear submarines."

"I remember Mom telling us about one of the nuclear

submarines going up the Columbia River many years ago," said Carly. "It was a big deal, and some of the school kids got to ride on a bus and go on the submarine while it was stopped in Portland."

"I'm sure that was a really exciting day for those kids," said Julia. "So, here's one interesting factoid: nuclear submarines can run thirty years or more on one refueling of uranium. They can stay underwater practically forever, or at least months at a time."

"I wouldn't want to be on one for that long," said Carly. "If people get island crazy in the Hawaiian Islands because they're confined to a finite space in the middle of an ocean, imagine what happens on a submarine."

"It would take a certain personality, for sure," said Julia.

"Uh, oh," said Carly, stopping in the hallway. "It looks like we have to be registered to get through the door."

She pointed to the official-looking man standing at the entrance. He had a clipboard to which he referred as each attendee stopped and gave a name. The gatekeeper then checked the identification badge and compared it to his list. He looked up and smiled as he checked off name after name.

"Excuse me, sir," said Julia when they were in front of him. "We're not registered, but we're interested in learning more about clean nuclear energy. Would it be okay if we sat in the back somewhere?" She smiled innocently.

"I'm sorry, miss, but this conference is restricted to those who paid to enter. I can't let you in." He smiled politely and dismissed them as he addressed the gentleman next in line.

"Good afternoon, Dr. Kennedy," he said. "Your seat is reserved in the second row. I'm looking forward to your talk."

"Thank you." He smiled and took a step.

Julia turned and asked as she recognized the man's voice.

"Beau? Beau Kennedy? It's me. Julia Fairchild. Biochemistry 405."

Beau stopped and stepped into the hallway where Julia stood with Carly. "Julia! What a surprise to see you, especially here." He gave her a quick, tiny hug. "What *are* you doing here?"

Julia smiled and shrugged. "It's kind of a long story, but it turns out we can't get in, after all."

"And who is 'we'?"

"Oh, forgive me. Let me introduce my sister Carly." They shook hands all around. "She and I are doing tourist stuff in Seattle—sort of a girls' week. Carly hasn't ever had a chance to spend any time here, and I wanted to do the things I couldn't afford or have time to do when I was in school."

Beau did a head bow toward Carly. "Nice to meet you. Julia and I had a few fun times when we were in school. I had to borrow her class notes more than once to study for an exam. She was the best note-taker." He turned to Julia. "Did you know that kids nowadays pay other kids to go to class and take their notes?" He shook his head.

"Doesn't surprise me. Some frat kid stole my microbiology notes just before the final exam when I was a student. I studied with some other friends who had notes, and I still did fine. My notes reappeared mysteriously about a week later. I hope he failed." Julia snorted.

"Would serve him right. Hey, the conference is about to start. I can get you in if you really want to stay for a while."

"Yes, please."

Beau turned back to the gatekeeper as Carly raised an eyebrow at Julia. Julia just shrugged back.

Beau talked to the man—maybe a grad student, Julia thought—then turned and waved Julia and Carly into the room.

"Thank you so much," Julia said sweetly as they entered the room. Beau pointed to a couple of seats about halfway up from the podium, then scooted to his own reserved place in the front. Julia noted that he was in full "professor dress" with jacket, shirt and tie, unlike the casual attire of most of the others.

The conference room was decorated in the typical utilitarian style: beige-gray paint on the walls, rows of seats with minimal padding that stretched out behind a long table that extended across the room, with an aisle in the center, pitchers of water with several cups placed about every fifth seat, and a couple of plastic bowls next to it filled with pretzels or wrapped candies. Julia had endured many a lecture in similar auditorium-style rooms.

Carly whispered, "I'm not sure why we're here. I'm sure you didn't plan to meet your old friend here."

Julia shook her head. "Of course not. I haven't seen him since college. That would be about twenty years ago now. Yikes! I'm getting old."

"So why are we here?"

"I'm curious about why our John Doe had that piece of paper in his hand. Maybe we'll learn something."

"We already told the detective. Maybe that piece of paper had nothing to do with him. And you promised we were done already."

"Let's learn something about clean nuclear energy." Julia winked at her sister, who sat back in her chair, rolled her eyes and crossed her arms.

CHAPTER

FIVE

The first lecture about comparing nuclear energy to carbon-based fuels was boring to Julia as well as to others in the audience, judging by the number of attendees whose eyes were closed and heads were leaning backward at awkward angles. Polite applause followed. During the break, Carly said, "I've heard enough. Can we leave now?"

Julia pulled out the schedule she'd been given at the room's entrance and pointed to the next topic, "Today's Nuclear Submarine," which would be covered by her friend Beau.

"Are we staying here because the lecture is being given by your friend?"

"No, not that. It's because of the piece of paper our mystery man had in his hand."

Carly sighed and relented to sit through the lecture. "But only one more boring talk."

Julia scanned the audience and watched as some of the people left and others filed in. Then she saw the three men who had been with their John Doe Saturday evening. They entered the room at the last moment, seconds before Beau's lecture was to begin. She poked her sister in the arm.

"What?" Carly whispered loudly.

Julia pointed to the three men, but the room's lights had already been dimmed. "I'll tell you when the lights come back on," she whispered back.

Beau's lecture was about the United States' nuclear submarine program and some changes that were being made to improve its efficiency and effectiveness. Most of what he said was nonspecific, but Julia found it particularly interesting when he referred to the *Sealab* experiments that had been done in the 1960s and later abandoned. He was an eloquent speaker, she thought; she didn't notice anyone nodding off.

A couple of questions were asked about nuclear safety on board; "very safe" was the answer. Another asked about whether there were nuclear weapons onboard the submarines and was assured there were none. Nuclear power was used exclusively to power the submarine. Generous applause followed, then it was announced that there would be a fifteen-minute break before the next lecture.

When the lights were turned on, Julia looked for the three gentlemen who had entered late but didn't see them anywhere. She mentally berated herself for not sneaking a photo of them earlier, but the darkness of the room would have prevented that, anyway.

"Dang," she said.

"Why did you poke me earlier?" Carly asked.

"I saw those three guys come in who were with the man at the taxi stand when we came out of "Spooked in Seattle." But now they're gone." Julia got up to leave with the crowd.

"Are you sure? I mean, that they were the same men?"

"Definitely. I recognized the profile of the nose of one of

them, and they were wearing the same jackets we saw Saturday night. Maybe they're in the hallway. Let's go."

They hurried as fast as they could, considering most of the audience was trying to leave at the same time through a single door.

Julia glanced up and down the hallway and didn't see any of them lolling about. "Missed them."

"I don't see how just seeing them here would help figure out anything," said Carly.

"I wanted to get a picture on my camera to send to Detective Monroe," said Julia. "I thought it might help."

"Have you already forgotten that we're not involved in solving this one?" Carly stood with one hand on a hip and a stern look on her face.

"It only would have been a picture," she said, with a look of chagrin on her face. She turned when she heard Beau call her name.

"Great lecture, Beau," Julia said as he approached them. "I was fascinated by your comments about the *Sealab* project. Is that something that's in the works again?"

Beau winked. "Of course, I can't say anything about what might be in the works. But how about a drink on me for both of you? I can meet you somewhere when I'm done for the day."

"We'd love that," said Julia.

Carly nodded with a smile, golden curls bobbing.

"Where are you staying? I can meet you nearby, perhaps."

"We're at the Edgewater. They have a bar there, or we could walk down the pier to—"

"I love the Edgewater. Meet you in their lobby about six?"

"Love it. See you then."

~

THE WEATHER WAS perfect for a leisurely walk back to the hotel. Other than having to be cautious when crossing the streets when the lights changed—some drivers forgot that there might be pedestrians in the sidewalks—they enjoyed the cacophony of the city and the late afternoon sun. Julia loved to visit Seattle for a few days, whether for a conference or a mini-vacation such as she was having with Carly. She didn't want to live in such a busy place, but for a few days, she enjoyed the experiences offered that didn't exist in her own small city of 40,000 or so.

She had lived in Seattle for four years while going to the university and felt familiar with its layout. She never felt lost there, unlike trying to drive in Portland, which was closer to her now but still presented a challenge every time she tried to find her way home from the downtown area. It seemed like her car's GPS gave her different directions every time.

Carly, on the other hand, had gone to college in a smaller town and now lived on the family farm. She was more used to cows and chickens and taking care of her ten acres on the hillside in the country.

"You didn't tell me how you know Beau—I mean, Dr. Kennedy," said Carly. "It was nice of him to let us into the lecture hall, even if that first expert was boring."

Julia put a little kick into her step. "We sat next to each other in a biochemistry class. It was a required course for pre-med students like me, as well as for some engineering students, depending on their major. I think he started in chemical engineering, or maybe it was biology. Anyway, we had a few dates and studied together that year. He was a senior, and I was a junior. Then he met Allison, and he fell head over heels for her. I didn't know her well—I met her a couple of times when she was with Beau, and we'd had an English class together as freshmen—but I remember that she came from a wealthy family and belonged to a sorority. I heard they'd gotten engaged after graduation. Anyway, I went off to medical school, and he went into grad school. And that was that."

"Hm. I got the feeling there's more to it than that. I did notice that he had a ring on his finger."

"Yeah. So?"

"So he's married."

"And?"

"I wonder if he'll tell his wife he's having drinks with an old girlfriend."

"A, I'm not an old girlfriend, and B, we're just having drinks. And C, you'll be there. Sheesh. We're not going to start an affair or anything."

"Just keeping an eye out for you, sis."

JULIA AND CARLY freshened up for their "date" with Beau. Julia felt grimy after the full day in the city. The walk had been refreshing in that they were outdoors, but it had also exposed them to car exhaust and the fumes of a big city. They arrived in the lobby a few minutes early and sat down to wait on a bench next to a window overlooking the water. The late afternoon sun streamed through the glass.

"I wonder why those three men were at the conference today," said Julia. "It looks like they may have come in only for the nuclear submarine discussion."

"You don't really know if that was their only lecture. We missed all the morning schedule."

"That's true. But they came in at the last second and left before the lights came back on. Like they didn't want anyone to notice them."

"You're probably reading more into this with that suspicious mind of yours, sis."

"Maybe, but if they were the trio who had been with the man we found at the arboretum, wouldn't you want to know more about them?"

"*I* wouldn't, but maybe the police would."

"I wonder if Detective Monroe found out anything else."

"No detecting. No *thinking* about detecting." Carly's eyes threw daggers at her sister.

Julia shrugged. "I wonder if Mr. John Doe has a name yet, or if he's awake." When she noticed Carly's glare, she said, "Just normal curiosity."

"Not normal for most people. Only for you."

CHAPTER
SIX

"There's Beau," said Julia, who had been keeping an eye on the massive wooden doors. She stood to greet him.

He nodded and said, "Hi, Carly," then hugged Julia and sneaked a little kiss on her forehead. "Hi, Julia." She blushed bright crimson under her sister's watchful eyes.

The drinks menu listed several cocktails with local names, as well as the standards. "I haven't tried them all, but everything I have had here has been quite good," said Beau. "I'm going to go with a Moscow Mule for now."

Carly said, "I'm eyeing that Spritz Kiss. I can't imagine what an elderflower liqueur tastes like."

"I'll try the Gas Works Flannel cocktail, and we can trade sip, if you like," said Julia to Carly.

"Tell me what you girls were talking about as you waited for me."

"Carly and I were talking about a trio of men who entered your lecture, then left before the lights came on. Did you notice them?"

"Can't say as I did, but when I'm in the front of a dark room, all I see are the lights from the projector and reflections off people's glasses. What about them?"

Julia looked at Carly. "Shall I tell him?"

Carly said, "I don't see why not."

"Now I'm really curious. What is it?"

Julia paused as the waiter took their drink orders.

Julia resumed talking and told Beau about seeing a quartet of men Saturday night after they'd been on the ghost tour, then finding one of them the next day at the arboretum. "He had obviously been injured somehow but was still alive. I haven't heard anything about him since."

"So, you see these men at my lecture and think it's suspicious? How? Why?"

Julia sighed. "What if they were responsible for his injuries?"

"This is Seattle. Maybe he was out by himself in a tough neighborhood and got beat up all by himself," said Beau.

Julia shook her head. "I don't see it. If I were a tourist or here for a conference, as it seems these guys are, I wouldn't be wandering around alone."

"You're not a guy." Beau smiled. "I've done it when I travel to conferences. I like to get a feel for the area, especially if I've never been there before."

The waiter appeared with a tray of drinks. "Cheers to old friends and new," said Beau, with a wink to Julia and a nod to Carly.

After a couple of swallows, Beau asked, "What did you two think of my lecture? Or did you find it as boring as the lecture before mine?"

"This Gas Works Flannel drink is potent," said Julia. "Try a sip, Carly, while I answer Beau's question." She coughed a couple of times as the liquor slid down her throat. "Admittedly, it was slightly over my head for the most part. But I really enjoyed the bit about how the Navy uses dolphins and sea lions to patrol some of the submarine bases, like Bangor."

Beau nodded, a smile on his face. "The average person wouldn't know anything about that, but there's a training program in San Diego. It's an extension of the program from the sixties, when a dolphin named Tuffy was used to ferry supplies from the *Sealab* chamber to the mother ship."

"That's amazing," said Carly. "Can you tell us how they're trained?"

"Not exactly, but I do know that about fifty dolphins and sea lions are being used at Bangor to patrol the four miles along the underwater coast."

"What are they trained to do?" asked Julia. "It's hard to picture how they react when they sense danger. Or is that classified information?"

"Not at all. Back in 2010, the U.S. Navy got authorization to use some dolphins and sea lions at Bangor. The dolphins patrol for two hours at a time, with a human handler. They have keen eyesight, like an eagle, and can see a rope in the water, for example, from about a mile away. They carry a beacon which they drop when they encounter an intruder such as a scuba diver. The beacon lets the Navy know where to go to intercept said diver. The dolphin often works with a sea lion that carries a special kind of soft clamp that it can attach to the diver's leg. Then the Navy divers take over."

"That's amazing," said Carly.

"Yes," said Beau. "These wonderful animals are trainable, loyal, and very effective. There are about eighty dolphins and fifty sea lions trained at any one time. Most of them are just north of us at Bangor, Washington, and in Georgia. The rest are in San Diego, where they're trained."

"That sounds a lot more advanced than the dolphin did in the old television series, *Flipper,*" said Julia.

"Yes," said Beau. "Back in the sixties, nobody knew the capabilities of these wonderful mammals. Over the years, the Navy has endured a lot of grief because the uninformed don't understand that the dolphins are cared for in a very humane way. Better than some humans, I would say."

"That's simply incredible. And most of us don't have a clue," said Julia.

"If I were a guy, I think I'd join the Navy myself and apply to be a SEAL," said Carly.

Julia chuckled. "You don't like boats, remember? How would you manage such a feat?"

"Fortunately, I don't have to make such a decision because I'm a girl and not a boy." Carly lifted her chin in the air.

Beau cleared his throat. "Carly, they take women in the SEALS program these days."

"Oh. Well, I'm too old for that now. Maybe in my next life-time." She blushed.

"Beau," said Julia, "the last time I saw you was when we were in college and you had started dating Allison. I see you have a ring on your finger. Is she the lucky woman?"

Beau glanced at his hand and nodded. "We've been married fourteen years already. Three kids—twin girls named Cecily and Rylie and a son, Benjamin. She's a remarkable woman and a great mother. I feel pretty fortunate."

Julia's phone buzzed. "It's a Seattle number. Excuse me for a minute while I take the call." Julia turned her head.

"Hello...Yes, this is Dr. Fairchild...Hi, Detective Monroe...We were just talking about that gentleman and were wondering if you had learned anything about him...nothing new? I might have something. I think we saw the three men he had been with Saturday...today at the Pacific Science Center...they sat in on a lecture about nuclear energy…just a minute. I'll have you talk to Dr. Beau Kennedy. It was his lecture."

Julia handed the phone to Beau. "It's the detective who came to the arboretum."

Beau got up from the table and moved closer to the window, out of Julia's earshot. She watched him from a dozen feet away but couldn't decipher the conversation. He appeared to be doing more listening than talking. He ended the call and handed the phone to Julia.

"Your detective friend said they haven't been able to identify your mystery man yet. He's still unconscious from a subdural hematoma—I think he called it—and hasn't even opened his eyes. His fingerprints aren't in any of the databases that they've checked, nor is his face in the system anywhere."

"A true John Doe," said Julia. "Was the detail about the others attending your lecture any help to him?"

"He pretty much dismissed the idea. And I wouldn't put much stock into it."

Julia took a long sip from her drink and passed it to Carly, who reciprocated with hers. "I just thought of something. There was the man with the clipboard at the entrance. Wouldn't the names of all the attendees be listed there? Can you find out, Beau?"

He furrowed his brow. "I can try, but no promises."

Carly asked, "How would you know which names belonged to them? If that man was simply checking names off from the list, he's probably not going to remember which of the attendees were the last three in the door."

Julia sighed, deflated. "It sounded like a good idea when I thought of it."

Beau chuckled. "I may be able to get the list of names, but Carly's right about being not able to determine which three names are the ones you want."

Julia sat with her chin on her hand, elbow on the table. "Tell you what. I'll give you my card, and you give me one of yours. Whoever finds out something can call and share what they know." Julia fished out her business card, adding her personal cell number.

"Do you have any plans for tonight, Julia?" asked Beau. "There's so much to do here it would be hard to choose."

"I think we'll go to the Laser Dome at the Seattle Center. I saw online that it is a descendant of the original Spacearium that was created for the World's Fair in the sixties." Julia furrowed her brows. "Hm. Interesting. The *Sealab* and the Spacearium were both created in the same decade—both in the sixties."

"What was the Spacearium?" asked Carly.

Julia read from an article she'd found on her phone. "This says it 'took up to 750 visitors on an imaginary ten-minute excursion to the outer galaxies.' I'm guessing they were in something like an IMAX theater."

Beau took the last sip of his drink, wiped his mouth, and said, "Interesting. Well, have fun." He took care of the bill when the waiter approached, then stood and said, "Thank you for favoring me with your company." To Julia, he said, "It was such a treat to see you today." He took her hand and kissed the back of it. "Nice to meet you, Carly. Keep that sister of yours out of trouble."

"This has been such a busy day," said Carly as she and Julia finished their drinks. "I'd rather just stay here at the hotel and eat, or we could go get pizza down the street at Pike Place Market."

"That's quite a long walk, and it's dark outside. There's an Anthony's practically next door, but I agree with you. I'd rather stay in and rest my feet until tomorrow."

"We can order room service, look at the list of things to do that we got from the concierge, and plan something for tomorrow while we eat pizza."

"Great idea."

"Thanks," said Carly, grinning. "Plus, I won't have to worry about you getting into trouble if you stay right here!"

Julia made a face at her sister. "I looked at the menu here. It's pretty fancy, with matching prices. What if we order a pizza to be delivered to us with Door Dash and eat it in our room? I brought a bottle of Chianti that will add just the right touch."

"Perfect."

PAJAMAS AND ROBES ON, wine glasses in hand, hot, thin-crust pepperoni and sausage pizza on the table, a *Blue Bloods* rerun on the television: a perfect night in. Julia and Carly feasted on the deliciousness until they were totally stuffed.

"Couldn't have done that in our pajamas at the pizza place," said Carly. "I'm full now, but I'll be ready to tackle the world tomorrow. What were you and Josh originally planning to do while he was here? Maybe we should go with that list."

Julia wriggled in her chair. "Well, *I* was supposed to come up with the list, but when he told me that he wouldn't be able to come after all, with the office transfer and all, I lost interest."

"Except you invited me, so you still should have made a list."

"I have a list in my head," said Julia. "Does that count?" She ducked as Carly pretended she was going to pour her wine on her. "Let's choose together. That will make it the most fun."

"I like that idea. Nice save." Carly picked up one of the lists from the concierge that had been compiled for guests and handed Julia a second one that they had picked up from a rack.

Carly thumbed through the first pamphlet. "What about riding the ferry to Bainbridge Island? I haven't done that since the days we visited our cousins in Winslow."

"That would be fun. I still have a pair of the Dutch shoes that Great Uncle Pat brought back from Holland years ago," said Julia. "Do you remember when we walked across the hardwood floor on our toes and then on our heels and left big black scuff marks because of the rubber soles?"

"Yeah, Mom was hopping mad, and we had to clean them up with a lot of elbow grease." After another couple of minutes, Carly said, "The Outdoor Sculpture Park would be nice on a dry day. We'll have to check the weather report first.

Or a Harbor Ferry cruise that leaves from Pier 65. Have you ever done that?"

Hearing no response, Carly glanced at Julia, who was staring out the window. "Carly to Julia, come in, please."

Julia shook her head. "Oh, I'm sorry. I wasn't paying attention. What did you say?"

"I said we should do the canoe ride again."

"What? Why?"

"Teasing. I suggested the Outdoor Sculpture Park or a Harbor Ferry cruise. What are you thinking about, anyway?"

"What if Beau looked at the roster for that session and identified the names of the people who *didn't* show up, even though they were registered? Maybe that would reveal the name of the John Doe."

"You're talking about the talk at the Science Center, I presume. Which is in the hands of the Seattle Police."

"Actually, they're not involved with that part. They only know about the guy with no name at the arboretum."

"Neither of which is your problem." Carly glared at her sister.

Julia took another sip of the wine. "I think we should tell Beau, and he could check it out. Since he was one of the presenters at the seminar, he likely has access to that list."

"That idea I can live with. Now, what do you want to do tomorrow?"

"Let's ride the ferry over to Bainbridge Island. I read somewhere that all the towns on the island voted in the early nineties to become one city named Bainbridge Island. And where the ferry landing is located is now called Eagle Harbor, which used to be Winslow."

"And if our cousins still lived there, it would be fun to call and visit, but I know they're scattered. I remember Mom telling us that Great Uncle Pat died years ago."

"We won't need ferry reservations to go as walk-ons. There's a nice shopping area just up the hill from where we land. And a couple of restaurants nearby. My high school classmates and I visited it about five years ago."

"Good to know." Carly retrieved her cell from the bed and checked the forecast. "The weather report looks ideal. Temperature in the sixties and no rain."

Julia got up from her chair and found Beau's business card. "I should call Beau tonight because he'll be teaching tomorrow, and it'll be harder to catch him."

He answered after two rings.

"Hi, Beau. Julia here."

"I know. I put your number in my contacts already. What's up?"

"I thought of another way to use the seminar roster to identify the John Doe, and I wanted to share my idea."

"Okay. What are you thinking?"

"Were you one of the organizers of that symposium?"

"Yes, and?"

"Well, two ideas came to mind. First one is to look at the roster for the lecture that you did on nuclear submarines and see if there is anyone who *didn't* show up. If the victim was buddies with the other three, maybe they all planned to go. That could help Detective Monroe narrow down the possible identification of the John Doe we found."

"He might not have been registered, Julia. You and Carly weren't, remember?"

"Let's operate on the assumption he *was* registered and didn't show up because he was in the hospital. Even if there were several other registrants who failed to show, it's somewhere for the police detective to start."

"Okay. I follow, but I think it's a long shot. What's your second idea?"

"One of your brainy computer people could do a comparison test of the seminar attendees and see if those three men attended other sessions or just the one on nuclear subs."

"I don't follow you on that one."

"I just have a hunch that the nuclear submarine topic is what connects the John Doe to the other men. So if there's a trio that attended *just* that session, it could be the men Carly and I saw Saturday night. The ones who were with the John Doe. I can't explain better than that."

"Hmm. One of my grad students, Laci Lia Ling, would be the best person to talk to. How about coming by my office tomorrow morning? Could you come by about eight? She's always there by then."

Julia shared Beau's proposal with Carly, got a nod, and said, "We can do that. Give me the details, and we'll see you in the morning."

"For someone who doesn't need to be involved, you're sure acting like this is your case," said Carly after Julia ended the call.

"It feels personal. That guy locked eyes with me and then showed up at our feet. How can I not feel like I should help?"

"Easy. Stay out of it and let Detective Monroe do his job."

"I will. After we meet Laci Lia Ling."

Carly harrumphed and picked up the book she'd started reading.

CHAPTER
EIGHT

Despite her best planning, by the time Julia negotiated morning traffic around the university, bribed the gate guard to let them park nearest the engineering building, and found an empty spot in the almost-full lot, it was a quarter past eight.

After consulting the list of offices next to the elevator, they found the door sign that read *Beau Kennedy, MS, Ph.D.* on the second floor. The door opened into an office where a smartly-dressed, fifty-ish woman sat behind a neatly organized desk. She looked up and smiled. "Can I help you?"

"Hello," said Julia. "We're looking for Dr. Kennedy. He invited us to meet him here. I'm Julia Fairchild, and this is my sister Carly Pedersen."

"And I'm Monica, the department secretary." She rose from her chair and said, "Follow me. He's in Ms. Ling's office next door." She held the door open for them and excused herself.

Beau and a young Asian woman were bent over a computer, heads very close together, when Julia and Carly entered the small space. After Beau made the introductions,

Laci Lia asked a couple of clarifying questions before saying she understood Julia's quest. Beau had already given her a brief explanation, it appeared.

She opened the seminar attendee master list and said, "This would take quite some time to sort manually, but I can enter this into a spreadsheet. It will do the work and have an answer for you in a couple of minutes." The pretty young woman smiled at Julia and said with a wink, "Anyone can do this."

"Thank you, Ms. Ling," said Julia. "I believe you mean anyone who knows how to use a spreadsheet."

Beau, standing behind Julia, laughed. "She's a whiz. Let me show you and Carly around the office while she does her magic."

As he walked down the sterile hallway of his department, he gave a brief history of how he ended up studying nuclear engineering when he decided to pursue a master's degree, followed by a Ph.D. "I still don't know all there is to know in the field because it has become much more complex as the world grows."

"Yes," said Julia. "Like having to choose a subspecialty in internal medicine once you've finished your basic three-year residency program."

"Why didn't you go on for more training?" asked Beau. "That seems like something you would have done."

"I had planned to go into gastroenterology, but the program I looked into didn't appeal to me. And it was in southern California." She sighed. "Another was in Houston, and I knew I didn't want to live there for two or three years. Basically, I was ready to practice medicine and put subspecialty training on hold. I knew I could always go back if I really wanted to. And I never wanted to. I love what I do."

Beau smiled. "And it shows." He gave her a quick one-arm

hug, then entered the third room on the left down the hall. He introduced the sisters to two more graduate students who were busy in front of their computers.

"This is Chase McGill," said Beau, standing behind the desk of a tall, slender, dark-haired man with a couple of days' worth of facial hair. "He's been here the longest and should finish his doctoral thesis next year unless he drags his feet much longer." Chase nodded with pursed lips but didn't say anything.

"The other young man is in his first year with us. Ian Thompson is from England. He's working with one of the assistant professors." Ian waved from his desk near the windows on the other side of the room. Julia and Carly smiled and returned the gesture.

As they walked back down the hallway, he said, beaming, "Laci Lia is my star. She speaks five languages and a couple of Chinese dialects. I hope we can entice her to stay here once she finishes her doctoral work."

"How long does that take?" asked Carly.

Beau cocked his head. "Anywhere from three to ten years. Or forever for some of the students if they have outside funding—which isn't unusual for students from Iran or China, for example. It also depends on what they ultimately want to do and how motivated they are. Laci Lia should finish in the next year or so. She might even beat Chase."

Julia laughed. "I remember my dad calling me a 'perpetual student' when we talked about the number of years it takes to finish medical school, then internship and residency, and even several more years after residency for a fellowship program, like cardiology or infectious diseases."

Laci Lia was waiting with her report when Beau and his guests entered her office. Julia noticed that the door next to Beau's office had a sign that read *Laci Lia Ling*. She had her own private office space, which struck Julia as unusual for a grad student, and even more so to have her name painted on the pebbled glass window. She hadn't noticed Chase's name on an office door.

"I know you hoped to be able to identify certain men who attended only Dr. Kennedy's lecture," she said, pointing to a thick printout of data on her desk. "I was not able to find a set of three names that met that specific criterion, I'm sorry to report." She had a serious expression on her face briefly, then smiled. "But this may still help you. I printed a list of those who were registered but didn't appear for the designated seminars."

Julia quickly scanned the list and nodded. "There are only a dozen names here." She scrunched her eyebrows. "We can potentially eliminate several of them by the fact they have obvious Asian or Middle Eastern names, and our John Doe is clearly Caucasian."

"You mean *Detective Monroe* can use the list to try to identify John Doe," said Carly.

Julia grinned at her sister. "Isn't that what I said?" To Laci Lia, she said, "Here's the detective's contact info if you would be so kind as to email this list to him."

Beau said, "I'll take care of that. Thank you, Laci Lia."

The trio walked back to Beau's office next door. "Thank you, Beau. I don't know if that information will help the detective, but it can't hurt," said Julia.

Beau asked, "What's on your agenda today? It's going to be sunny and clear again, according to the weather forecast this morning."

"We thought we'd take the ferry over to Bainbridge Island and see what's changed since visiting our cousins there twenty-five years ago."

"A *lot* has changed," said Beau. "You wouldn't believe the

property values over there nowadays compared to when it was mostly small farms and country living. I wish I could join you, but I'm teaching most of the day."

"That would have been fun," said Julia. "I'm going to email an explanation of the list you're sending to the detective. Then I'll let you know what I find out after Monroe gets his hands on those names."

Beau gave Julia one more hug and nodded at Carly before escorting them to the elevator down the hall.

Once they were out of the building, Carly said, "He wasn't wearing his ring today. He had it on when we met him at the bar."

"Oh? I didn't notice."

CHAPTER

NINE

Because of the early morning meeting with Beau at his office, it was ten a.m. before Julia and Carly caught the ferry. It wasn't crowded because they'd missed the busier traffic of the commuters to Bainbridge and beyond. The sisters took station on the top deck and stood against the rail, the breeze fanning their faces, as they headed west across the water. They had decided to take Julia's car after all in case they wanted to drive around and check out the real estate. Or find their cousins' former home.

The Seattle weather was perfect for the morning crossing on the ferry to the island. Bainbridge Island had long been a suburb of sorts for Seattle. Many of its residents used the excellent Washington State Ferries system to commute across Puget Sound to work in Seattle during the week and enjoyed their idyllic island life the rest of the time. It was equally easy to take the bridge from the opposite side of the island to commute to work in cities such as Bremerton on the western side of Puget Sound. The ferry also made it easy to go to more remote cities on the Olympic Peninsula, such as Port Townsend and Port

Angeles. From there, many of the locals used the ferry system to hop over to Victoria, British Columbia.

"You do realize, I assume, that we don't have a clue as to where Butch, Patsy and Punky lived all those years ago," said Carly. "I only remember that they lived on a little farm and that Patsy rode horses at a stable somewhere."

"I remember that she had actual riding boots and rode Eastern style," said Julia. "I was jealous of those boots."

"I doubt they would have been useful riding bareback on Blossom. She hated being saddled."

"And they wouldn't have been practical when we were riding Picante. It seems like the corral was always muddy." Julia sighed. "But none of that mattered to me then. I was only eight or nine at the time."

"We may as well head to the car," said Carly, checking her watch. "I hate getting caught in a mad scramble down those stairs at the last minute."

Because they were riding the ferry in the opposite direction of the morning rush hour traffic, the car deck had room to spare. Julia felt a familiar thrill as she followed the hand signals of the men who directed the traffic as it left the ferry. For some reason, she loved riding the ferries. She maneuvered her Infiniti coupe one lane over to follow the car in the center lane, and drove up the ramp to the ferry landing pier. Carly pointed toward the sign that directed them to Eagle Harbor, formerly known as Winslow.

Julia joined the train of cars going the same way. "Hey, there's a sign that says Fletcher Bay. I kinda remember that as being closer to where our cousins lived."

"Do you think you're just going to drive around and miraculously stumble onto their old house? How would we even know if we found it?"

"I don't expect to find it, but I want to do more than just

check out the shops in town. Can you check the map from the concierge to see how far it is?"

Carly wrestled with the paper map for a moment. "The island is only five miles wide, so it can't be more than three or four miles from here, but I don't see a road that goes straight to it."

"That's okay. Let's head that way and admire the scenery. Maybe we'll find somewhere for lunch while we're over there. Then we can head back to town and window shop before we catch a ferry back. Does that sound okay?"

"Sure. I'll check my White Pages App while you're driving. Maybe I'll get lucky and find a number for one of the boys. They'll be easier because men don't usually change names when they get married. I know Patsy got married and was living in North Dakota last time Mom mentioned her. I don't remember her married name, anyway, even if she did move back here."

Julia engaged her NAV system and found Fletcher Bay, which lay to the west. She activated the route on her GPS and follower State Route 305 in a northerly direction until it intersected with High School Road, which headed generally westward.

"There are so many businesses and houses here now," said Julia. "It was all green trees and small farms thirty years ago."

"You know, the same thing is happening around our old farm. People are selling their acreage, whether it's ten or forty acres, to developers, or splitting them into smaller parcels and selling the lots themselves."

"I know. And I wish we could reverse that trend, but that's not happening." She glanced at her sister with her lips set in a straight line.

"No listings for our cousins in the local area," said Carly. "If they still live around here, they probably have cell phones, but I don't know how we'd ever track down a number."

"No biggie. It was just a thought."

As soon as they were clear of the main part of the town itself, the scenery changed to the green trees and small fields of Julia's memory. "This is more like it," she said. "Even the air seems fresher here."

She had barely made that comment when the scenery changed back to homes and a few businesses. She followed Fletcher Bay Road, then Miller Road northwest until they could finally see the water of Fletcher Bay.

"Hey. Do you see a park or some kind of access to the water on the map?"

"It looks like the bay is surrounded by homes for the most part," said Carly. "And I doubt anyone's going to invite us into one of these homes with a private dock."

"I haven't seen much in the way of places to eat either," said Julia. "Shall we head back to the other side and check out Rolling Bay? That's where Great Uncle Pat lived."

"He was such a kick. It took me years to figure out how he was related to us."

"I think his dad was married to our great-grandmother's twin. He would have been our mom's uncle, I guess. I always thought he was fooling with us about being our Irish uncle. But he really was, in a way—by marriage, at least."

Carly chuckled. "I remember his white hair and big mustache. Rolling Bay is back on the other side of the island. We can go east on New Brooklyn Road, then catch Sportsman Club Road and head north. It's going to be another residential neighborhood, but that's okay."

"We can see how the wealthy people live," said Julia.

The traffic was moderate on the drive across the midsection of the island to the eastern shore. "I'm going to take that road to Manitou Beach Park," said Julia. "I'm determined to put my foot in the water somewhere."

Julia's phone rang. Detective Monroe's name flashed on her car's screen.

"Hello. This is Julia."

"Detective Monroe from Seattle Police calling. Do you have a minute?"

"Sure. My sister is here, too. We're in the car, but I'm connected via Bluetooth."

"Fine. As you might have guessed, we've been keeping a guard outside our John Doe's hospital room. No reports of any people attempting to enter without permission. The good news is that today's guard just called to tell me that the man has finally awakened."

"That's good news. Does he have a name yet?"

"Unfortunately, no. His head injury was severe enough that he has no memory of anything other than eating dinner with some men in downtown Seattle. He can't tell us which restaurant, or what day, or names of any of his colleagues."

"Does he have an accent?" asked Julia. "Or is he an American?"

"That turns out to be rather interesting. Although he's Caucasian by looks, he spoke Chinese to the nurse. Fortunately, she was able to interpret for the detective who went in to try to interview him."

"Chinese?"

CHAPTER

TEN

"Yes, Chinese. The nurse told the detective that Mr. Doe seems to understand English when she talks to him but only answers in Chinese."

"That's strange. It makes me wonder if Chinese was his first language," said Julia. "Our mom's first language was Finnish, and I remember when she was in the ICU one time after surgery, the nurses couldn't understand her when she talked. I went up to see her and realized what was happening. She wouldn't respond to me in English either, just Finn. I had to call my dad to find out how to tell her to cough in Finnish. That lasted for a few days, but she finally shook off the effects of the anesthesia and opioids and talked normally again. That was a relief!"

"Maybe he's on pain meds, Julia," said Carly.

"I wouldn't be surprised, but with head injuries, physicians tend to use the minimal amount necessary to avoid this very problem," said Julia. "He has a subdural hematoma, which is blood between the skull and the brain, and causes pressure on the brain itself. It'll go away by itself, and there isn't any way to hurry it along."

"I'll check with the nurse about meds," said Detective Monroe, "but Julia's right. That's the same thing the doctor explained to me earlier."

"Changing subjects," said Julia. "What about the security cameras in the area around the "Spooked in Seattle" tour site? Anything there?"

"Sorry to say, no. There was one functional camera a half block away, but it was too grainy to be helpful."

"Drat," said Julia. "A dead end. At least for now."

"I'll stay in touch," said Monroe. "And thank you for the lists of names from Dr. Kennedy. I'll have our analyst take a look at them."

Julia had pulled to the side of the road during the call because she wasn't familiar with the area and didn't want the distraction to cause her to have an accident. Before pulling back into traffic, she asked Carly, "Do you want to keep going to that park or are you ready to head back?"

"I'm scenery'd out. The water's going to be cold today, anyway. It's only early May."

"Okay. I'll pull a U-turn here and head back toward the shops. I'm really hungry, by the way. Can you find a decent restaurant between here and the ferry landing?"

Carly scrolled through the options on her phone. "Aha! This one looks good. It's called the Bainbridge Brewing Alehouse. Keep heading toward the ferry and make a right turn on Winslow Way in a couple of miles." She grinned at her sister. "Can't miss it."

"What's on the menu?" Julia asked. "I want real food."

"Let's see—uh, oh. They only have snack foods. Keep going while I find something else."

Julia let her mind wander back to the still-unidentified

man at the hospital. Could he have been raised in China with missionary parents? Was he a student of the Chinese language? Or...? She shook her head. They could only hope he regained full consciousness in time.

"Here's a better choice. The Harbor Public House is next to the marina and has beer and real food. And good prices. Turn right on Winslow Way, then left onto Madison Avenue and right on Parfitt Way. Never mind. I'll set my GPS and tell you when to turn as we go. We'll be there in about fifteen minutes, I think."

THE PUB RESTAURANT was at the end of a cul-de-sac. Luckily, the main part of the lunch hour was already over, which meant a couple of street-side parking spots were available nearby. Lively music and loud voices trying to be heard over the noise filled the air when Carly opened the door.

"Looks good. Smells delicious," Carly said as she sniffed the air. "They've got hamburgers, for sure."

They headed for a high-top table near the window. "I think this table is a little farther away from the speakers," said Julia, pointing to the boxy units hanging from the beams on the other side of the room.

After ordering a draft IPA for Julia and a hefeweizen for Carly, they studied the menu.

"I can't resist a good clam chowder," said Julia, licking her lips.

"I'll test the fish and chips," said Carly. "There's a comment about their french fries that makes me want to try them. I'll share."

Julia shared her ruminations about why John Doe—or maybe he was "Zhang San," the Chinese equivalent—might speak Chinese instead of English or another language. "We don't know if he's American. He could be from Europe, or even Russia or any other country, with his Caucasian looks."

"Detective Monroe is working on it," said Carly. "You're on vacation. And so am I."

Julia harrumphed. "Here's our food. Cheers."

Their window overlooked the busy marina. Sailboats and powerboats moved in and out of view as they traversed the harbor.

"Yum. Good food and good view. Nice choice, sister," said Julia.

"Here're the fries I promised to share," said Carly, reaching across the table. She sneaked a spoonful of chowder as payment in return.

THE FERRY WAS WAITING at the dock when they pulled up to the line of cars waiting for the return trip. "Good timing," said Julia. "I don't usually get that lucky. Let's go back up top and watch the Seattle skyline as we head back to civilization."

The thirty-five-minute ride went quickly. Julia followed Carly through the seating area toward the car deck when the intercom announced the impending landing. She grabbed the back of Carly's jacket and stopped walking when she saw a man who looked like one of the three from the lecture on the opposite side of the main lounge. "Carly. Look to your right. Isn't that one of the mystery men?"

"What mystery men?" Carly replied as she turned to look where Julia pointed. "Oh, *those* men." She paused and squinted her eyes. "Could be, but what are we going to do about it?"

Julia already had her phone out and had taken a couple of

photos. She quickly moved her phone out of sight when the man turned his face toward her.

"I think he was speaking Chinese, or some Asian language," said Julia. "I don't think he saw me, and I'm not sure it *was* one of them after I saw his face."

"As far as we know, the only person for sure who saw us was the unconscious man in the park," said Carly. "Right now, I'm very glad of that."

"I'll send these photos to Detective Monroe just in case. Maybe his face is in one of those databases like they have on *NCIS*," said Julia.

"And we're not going to try to follow them off the ferry, dear sister."

"If we can get a license plate number, that would be good enough."

"Except they could be walk-ons and not be in a car. And it's probably a rental if they are."

"You keep bursting my bubble, you know."

CHAPTER
ELEVEN

Julia lost sight of her prey when they entered the stairwell to go to the car deck. She and Carly hurried down the stairs for an opportunity to see the man emerge from the stairs, but it was not to be.

"Dang!" Julia said as they approached her car, still keeping her eyes on the stairway door. "Either he and his friends—at least I assume he was talking to someone he knows—are walk-ons and went to the lower deck, or are in a car parked down there."

"At least you have a photo to send to the detective. It might help, like you said, if he's in a database."

"We'll watch for him in the foot traffic when we get off. The pedestrians always get to disembark first, and maybe we'll be lucky enough to see him with his buddies getting into a car or taxi."

Sometimes it seemed to take forever to get off the ferry, especially when in a relative hurry, as was Julia's current situation. And even longer if parked on the upper auto deck, as was also the case. By the time it was her turn to drive up the ramp to exit the vessel, the foot traffic had evaporated into the atmosphere.

She asked Carly, "Do you see him anywhere?" Julia had to focus on the traffic and rely on her sister's eyes.

"Nary a soul to be seen. Even all the taxis are gone. Do you want me to forward that photo for you while you drive?"

"It feels good to stretch my legs after so many hours in the car," said Carly as they walked down the sidewalk toward Anthony's restaurant, where they had decided to have dinner. "That traffic coming back from the ferry was intense. I was really glad you were driving instead of me. Having never lived in a city bigger than Bellingham, and only when I was in college, I had no idea what city traffic is really like."

"Did you have a car? I don't remember any of us having one in college."

"Not me. I rode home with one of the other students."

"Same here. I had to ride the train home from the main Seattle train station to Parkview if I couldn't get a ride with someone. But that was way better than taking the Greyhound bus because it made a million stops and took twice as long."

Julia took a breath of the salty air. "It's nice to be able to walk to Anthony's from the Edgewater Inn. I was ready to park the car and forget about driving anywhere tonight for dinner."

The maître d' seated Julia and Carly at a table next to a window. The early evening sky was beginning to darken, and lights from the harbor traffic grew brighter as the day's last light disappeared. Julia sat with her chin on the heel of her hand, gazing at the view. "I never tire of looking at water. There's something about how the surface moves with the wind and the tide and the lights bounce off the waves that makes it mysterious and intriguing."

"How so?"

"It's like scuba diving. When the boat is at the surface and you look over the side, you can't tell what you're going to see thirty or fifty feet below you. It remains a surprise until you've entered the water and get closer to your target, whether it's a reef or shipwreck." Julia sighed. "You might see sea anemones or octopi or sea cucumbers or a treasure chest."

"Or a dead scuba diver, like you did when you went to St. Maarten."

"That *was* a real mystery. I'd rather find a treasure chest next time."

"I presume you mean a real one, not like the fake pirate chests we saw in Virgin Gorda."

Julia nodded. "See what I mean? Being around water seems to be full of mysteries."

"You can make a mystery out of anything." Carly groaned. "We need to decide what to order, sis. Here comes the waiter with the wine."

"I absolutely adore crab cakes." She read from the menu. "These are served with a ginger-plum sauce and beurre blanc and are accompanied by coconut Jasmine rice. That sounds interesting. What are you choosing?"

"I'll try the Mahi Mahi. Since I won't be going to Hawaii anytime soon, I'll settle for eating my favorite fish. Next to salmon, of course."

"Of course. I won't tell Rob you said that about Mahi Mahi."

"And you're treating, so I don't have to worry about the price." Carly giggled. "The menu says it's served with a mild red curry sauce and Jasmine fried rice. Yum. My mouth is watering already."

"Here's to a lovely dinner in a fantastic restaurant with excellent company," said Julia, raising her glass.

Carly lifted her glass of chilled pinot grigio to Julia's glass. "Cheers to that." She took a sip. "This is a very nice wine."

"That might be why people keep coming back to Anthony's. I've eaten in at least half a dozen of their locations, myself."

"And the food, I'm sure. Hey, are you surprised you haven't heard from Monroe yet? I thought he'd get right on that list of names," said Carly.

"Not really. The Seattle police department likely has a slew of cases to work on at any one time. I had really hoped Laci Lia would have been able to narrow that list to fewer people."

"About that. She and Beau seemed pretty chummy when we saw them this morning. And I know he was wearing his ring when we saw him for drinks. Why does he take it off at work?"

"Did you notice his hand at the seminar?"

"No, but I'll bet he didn't have it on. Just a hunch."

"Hm," said Julia. "A guy taking his ring off always seems suspicious to me. It makes me wonder if he's having an affair." She looked at Carly with an arched eyebrow. "But it's not really any of our business."

Their meal arrived shortly, and the sisters dived in with gusto.

"This is divine," said Carly after her first few bites.

"Heavenly," said Julia.

"And we each have good company," said Carly, with a smile.

"Thinking of company, as in John Doe's companions at that tour," said Julia with a furrowed brow, "I wonder if Detective Monroe was able to identify the man in the picture I took on the ferry today."

"Do you suppose the detective is on duty this late?"

Julia shook her head. "Even police detectives get to go home eventually. I'll call him in the morning and ask him about the photo. He'll probably visit the hospital tomorrow and could show it to our victim then."

"*Our* victim? You mean *their* victim, right?"

Julia ignored the question and said, "Let's order dessert."

CHAPTER

TWELVE

"What should we do tomorrow, Carly?" Julia and her sister were sprawled on the bed after dinner. Carly was sending a message to her husband, Rob. Julia was checking clinic email on her laptop. "After we call Monroe, that is."

"The Harbor Ferry Ride looks interesting, but I'd rather stay on land," she replied after finishing her email. "What about going to the world-famous Pike Place Market? We can watch the fish flying through the air as I've seen in the commercials." Carly mimed tossing a fish with her pillow, which landed on Julia's back. "Oops."

Julia threw the pillow back but missed her sister. "Sounds good. We still haven't seen the laser show at the Seattle Center. That could be our evening entertainment."

"I'd love to see one of those shows. I just checked out one of the videos on YouTube, and it was amazing."

Julia's phone buzzed. "It's Beau. I wonder what he wants." She moved to a cushy chair next to the window and pulled up her knees. "Hi, Beau. Did you learn something new?"

"Maybe. I shared the nuclear energy conference attendee names with one of my friends who works for the Nuclear Regulatory Commission. Something you said about the word 'nuclear' being highlighted on that scrap of paper made me wonder if he would know anything more."

"And?"

"Chip—Chip Englund, my friend— just got back to me. He said he'd seen the name of one of them on a list of attendees at another conference not long ago."

"What conference was that?"

"It was a symposium that included an update on the use of nuclear power in submarines. Chip remembers this guy because he asked a ton of questions about *Sealab*."

"*Sealab*? Isn't that an outdated topic?"

"Yes," said Beau, "generally speaking, but there was a documentary produced a few years ago and a book several years earlier that seem to have spiked an interest in the topic."

"Did your friend Chip say what kind of questions they were?"

"No, but he said the speaker had done extensive reading about the project and made himself an expert of sorts."

"Hm," said Julia. "Which might explain why Mr. X was asking the questions of that particular expert. But doesn't explain his avid interest in those old experiments."

"True. I don't know if you're interested or not, but Chip is in town until tomorrow. Would you like to meet him? I mentioned your mysterious John Doe to him, and he'd love to talk with you. And your sister."

"Let me check with Carly. We're planning our adventures for tomorrow, and maybe we could fit it in after we visit Pike Place Market."

"Actually, I was hoping you could meet him tonight if it's not too late for you."

"Fit what in?" Carly looked up from her novel, the mystery by Louise Penny that Julia had given her and that she'd finally started.

"Beau asked if we could meet his friend Chip, who works for the Nuclear Regulatory Commission and is only in town till tomorrow. He wants to meet us tonight."

"I guess we could do that," said Carly with a shrug.

"Ok, Beau. Where shall we meet him?"

"How about letting me pick you and Carly up at the hotel in about twenty minutes? I'll pick Chip up on my way there and take all of you out to Ray's Boathouse at Shilshole."

"That sounds great. I haven't been there in years. Meet you in the lobby."

"I suppose I should put nicer clothes on," said Carly. "Pajamas might not meet the dress code."

"Same here," said Julia.

"What else did Beau say? I only heard your half of the conversation."

Julia shared what she had learned. "I should have asked if Chip said anything about the man's nationality. Well, we can ask him when we see him. And we can also ask him about that expert speaker on the *Sealab* experiments."

"I don't get what the big deal is about that old project," said Carly. "Nuclear submarines have been around since the early fifties, haven't they? And nuclear energy is used by many countries around the world."

"True and true. The only clinker here is that a man we found almost dead and still doesn't have a name was with some men who went to a symposium on nuclear submarines. And he speaks Chinese. Why?"

"You might be reading too much into this whole thing. If we hadn't seen him after that tour downtown Saturday night, he would be an ordinary John Doe."

"Not really," said Julia. "He had that bit of paper in his hand about the nuclear talk."

"Oh. Right."

"I keep kicking myself for not doing something when I saw him that first time. Maybe all this would have been prevented," Julia said as she sorted through her clothes to find something proper to wear.

"And exactly what do you think you could have done? All he did was look at you."

"I could have taken a photo of the cab and the license plate number."

"Julia, how could you possibly have known that he was going to be a victim of anything? There's nothing you could have done at the time to change the outcome." Carly held up a fuchsia-colored top and black pants. "This outfit should do."

"The taxi company would have records of where the driver dropped them off."

"As I said, it wouldn't have changed anything."

The Tuesday evening crowd at Ray's Boathouse at the Shilshole Marina was on the small side. Beau had asked for a table in a quiet corner. The maître d' accommodated him with a familiarity that suggested Beau was a regular visitor.

Beau introduced Julia and Carly to his friend Chip Englund and ordered a bottle of wine and a charcuterie tray for the table.

Chip was a pleasant man in his fifties. He was balding with gray-tinged hair and blue eyes and appeared to be reasonably fit despite a little paunch. His attire—gray slacks and navy blazer—screamed *engineer*. If he had worn a tie earlier in the day, he had already removed it and opened the top button of his light-blue shirt, revealing a standard white crew-neck T-shirt. Julia couldn't tell if he had a plastic pocket protector for pens in the shirt pocket.

"I understand you two had some kind of interaction with a man who attended a conference where I was one of the speakers a few months ago," said Chip. "Please tell me what you know."

"It's not much," said Julia. "We, Carly and I, happened to notice a group of men at a tour downtown Saturday night. One of them looked right at us. I knew in my gut that something was wrong. Then they left in a taxi."

"Why did you think there was something wrong?" asked Chip.

Julia pursed her lips. "He had a strange look on his face, like he'd seen a real ghost. And it looked like they pushed him into the taxi."

"But the tour was *about* ghosts," said Carly, "so I—we—thought at first it was from something he'd seen there. Except he came from the alley and not from the bar where the ghost tour ended."

"It wasn't until the next day when we found that same man unconscious in the arboretum that we knew something really *was* wrong," said Julia. "A scrap of paper under his hand was the only clue about him." She told Chip the other details and how she and Carly had gone to the symposium at the Seattle Science Center as a result. "That's where we ran into Beau."

They stopped talking while the waiter served the appetizers and poured the wine—a French viognier, Julia noted.

After properly toasting the lovely May weather and tasting the delicious wine, Chip began the background of his interest in Julia and Carly's observations. "I understand you already know a little bit about the *Sealab* experiments that were done in the sixties. *Sealab One, Two,* and *Three* were experimental underwater habitats developed by the United States Navy to study the viability of saturation diving and humans living in isolation for extended periods of time."

"Didn't they already know something from submarine environments? They were already in use during World War Two," said Julia. "This brie is yummy, by the way."

Chip nodded. "Yes, but these later underwater studies were more in-depth. Ultimately, the knowledge gained from the *Sealab* expeditions helped advance the science of deep-sea diving and rescue and contributed to understanding the psychological and physiological strains humans can endure."

"Okay," said Carly. "Then why were they stopped? Did they learn what they wanted to know?"

"A few unrelated but well-publicized problems put a stop to the experiments. There were problems with sabotage of the air supply from the support ship during decompression at one point. They also had problems with the constant cold environment, which was related to the use of helium. Later, a poor gasket seal allowed helium to leak into the chamber in *Sealab Three*. One of the aquanauts died when the four divers tried to repair the leak while underwater instead of getting the unit back to the surface as quickly as possible."

"Ouch," said Carly. "Bad publicity. Just like when astronauts die during an explosion after launch into space."

"Yes. Plus, they were millions of dollars over budget and eighteen months behind schedule. The Navy finally killed the project."

"What happened to the chambers after the program was stopped?" asked Carly.

"From what I learned when I was doing my research, *Sealab Two* and *Three* used the same chamber, four years apart, after it had been refurbished. When the experiments were ended in 1969, the Navy retrieved the chamber and eventually dismantled it. *Sealab One,* the first of the projects, had been used in the waters off Bermuda Island. It was retrieved relatively intact, and is now on display outdoors at the Museum of Man in the Sea in Panama City Beach, Florida. The exterior was restored in 2014 and was painted in its original colors as part of the fiftieth anniversary of *Sealab.*"

"That would be pretty cool to see," said Carly.

"I still don't understand why the interest in *Sealab* now," said Julia.

Chip asked quietly, "Do you know anything about Jim Creek?"

CHAPTER

THIRTEEN

Julia and Carly looked at each other, shaking heads, then back at Chip.

"Who or what is 'Jim Creek'?" asked Julia. "It sounds like a man who might have been a pioneer, or even a Native American."

Chip chuckled. "It's a 'what.' Jim Creek is the location of the powerful transmitter the U.S. Navy uses to communicate with its submarines, among other things, anywhere in the world."

"How is that possible?" asked Julia. "I can barely get the Seattle radio stations sixty miles south of here."

"First, it's very powerful—1.2 million watts. Second, it uses a very low-frequency signal that is significantly lower than normal radio signals. It can transmit messages to the seven seas."

"What about underwater? I heard you say submarines."

"Yes, underwater, too," he replied, nodding. "But please don't ask me to explain it."

Julia laughed. "I really don't understand AM or FM signals,

although I know what the letters stand for. I'm sure I wouldn't have a clue even if you did explain it."

Carly snickered. "They don't teach that in medical school? And here I thought you knew everything."

Julia made a face at her sister and asked, "What's the big deal with Jim Creek right now?"

"A couple of years ago, one of Russia's high-level broadcasters made some comments on television about 'Jim Creek' being a potential target for Russian attacks. Or course, that kind of comment is scrutinized carefully, but, at the time, there wasn't any other indication of imminent action on the part of the Russians."

"And how would we know if such an action were being planned?" Julia finished her glass of wine, which Beau obligingly refilled. "Although I'm sure our government has its ways."

"Exactly," said Chip. "Maybe you've heard about chatter that goes on in the background and on underground circuits. That kind of talk is constantly monitored by us, by the Russians. Even by the Chinese."

"Okay, and...," said Julia.

"And recently, our specialists have detected an unusual number of attempts to hack into the cybersecurity system at the Jim Creek center."

"An attempt isn't the same as an actual hack, is it?"

"No, but this is a new pattern, and it's from an unusual source."

"I'm not following you," said Julia.

"The signals are being traced to *Sealab*."

"Huh? You just told us *Sealab* was dismantled years ago."

"Exactly. Someone has been able to disguise their signal to appear as though it's coming from our own project. Except it's *Sealab Four*."

Beau coughed. Chip finished his wine.

Carly said, "Wow."

Julia asked, "How is that possible? There were only three *Sealabs*, right?"

Chip nodded. "The cyber hackers use methods similar to those used to trick you into thinking your credit card company needs your password when it's really a hacker who is hoping you'll fall for the line."

"I would think they would be ultra-sophisticated," said Julia. "But these guys have to know that *Sealab Four* doesn't exist, so why would they use that as a tagline now?"

"That's the 100 million dollar question, Julia. And we just don't know yet."

"Aha," said Julia. "That's why you're interested in the men we saw at the Space Center symposium a few days ago. Right?"

"Basically, yes. One of the names Beau forwarded to me was on a list of registrants for another lecture recently. I'm sure he was the one who asked about the *Sealab* project presented by another colleague in the field."

Carly asked, "Why can't you just locate this guy and interrogate him?"

Chip raised an eyebrow. "There's a problem. Every one of the names we tested against our database turns out to be false. We don't have any idea who he really is."

"So, you're hoping we somehow have a photo that matches up to one of your hacking suspects. Is that right?" asked Julia.

Chip's face reddened. "Uh, yes."

"Did you ever show Beau the picture of the man we found on our canoe ride?" asked Carly. "If he was interested in the nuclear submarine lecture, maybe Beau knows him. Or Chip might recognize him."

"I thought I did, but maybe not." Julia rummaged in her purse for her phone and pulled up the image. "Do either of you know who this is?" She passed her phone to Beau, who gave it a cursory glance before handing it to Chip, who did the same thing.

"Nope," said Beau.

"Me neither," said Chip, returning the phone to Julia's outstretched hand.

Julia noticed the narrowed brows as Chip looked at Beau. He opened his mouth as if to say something to Beau but kept his thoughts to himself for the moment.

"I'm sure it's not the same guy who asked those questions at the other conference," said Chip, finally.

"Oh, I just remembered that we saw a man on the ferry today," said Julia. She scrolled to the photo and handed it to Beau. "Does he look familiar? This might be one of the three men we saw after "Spooked in Seattle" Saturday night. But I'm not sure of it."

"What about the other two men?" asked Chip. "Were they there, too?"

Julia shook her head. "I only saw this man, but I heard some Chinese or Asian language in the background near him. Of course, I don't know if they came from his acquaintances or other ferry riders who have nothing to do with this."

Beau and Chip scrutinized the photo and handed the phone back to Julia.

"He's not anyone I know," said Beau.

"Nor do I know him," said Chip.

Julia asked Chip, "Is this the kind of thing that your agency would be delving into? Do you have the capability of digging into the underground and identifying him?"

Chip chewed on his lip. "Yes, and no. In theory, it can be done, but I would have to have more evidence than a photo of an unknown man to request additional searching of other databases."

"Even with the word *Sealab* being tossed around? That should trigger somebody's concern," said Julia.

Chip smiled, sat back in his chair, and picked up his refilled glass of wine. "There are a lot of crazies out there who ask about it from time to time. It seems there are some sci-fi authors, for example, who create underwater worlds for their universe. Besides, anyone can pick up a copy of the book that was written in 2012 or track down the documentary film that originally aired on Public Broadcasting System in 1969. There was also a more recent documentary movie called *American Experience: Sealab* that came out in 2019. The film doesn't have much technical detail, but it is interesting to watch."

"So, you aren't seeing this person as a serious concern?" asked Julia. "Just another incident of casual interest in a dead program?"

"Until there's more information, yes."

"Okay. That's good to know," said Julia. "I guess I won't worry about having to know where the closest underground shelter is just yet."

Beau laughed. "Julia, those shelters go back to the fifties and sixties! How do you even know about them?"

Julia shrugged. "I remember our parents talking about them. And there was a bit about the Cold War in our United States history classes."

Carly giggled. "More like ancient history, if you ask me."

Chip nodded and said, "You're right, Carly—ancient history. My point remains that our experts haven't detected any immediate threat, despite the chatter."

CHAPTER
FOURTEEN

"First thing to do is call Detective Monroe," Julia announced as she and Carly got ready for their outing Wednesday morning.

"Monroe," the detective said after one ring. "Do you have something for me, Dr. Fairchild?"

"Good morning, sir. Maybe," she replied. "Yesterday on the Bainbridge Island ferry, we saw one of the guys from Saturday night. I managed to sneak a picture of him. If the other men were with him, I didn't see them. We sent you the one photo that I did get after we got off the ferry. Oh, and I heard someone near him say something in an Asian-sounding language. But he was out of my sight. And I don't know for sure if he was talking to the guy in the picture or not, now that I think about it."

"Okay. Is that all? I haven't done anything with the picture yet."

"Carly and I were thinking that it would be interesting to see if your John Doe recognized the man in the photo. If he's still in the hospital and still confused, it might trigger something he remembers from that night."

"I like that idea," said Monroe. "I'll go over myself and test him. Last I heard, he still had amnesia and was still speaking Chinese."

"I was wondering about that," said Julia. "Thanks for the update."

Julia gave Carly a *Cliff's Notes* version of the conversation while they Ubered over to the world-famous Pike Place Market. Too many blocks to walk, Carly had announced.

"Wouldn't it be interesting if that picture *did* cause a reaction of some kind?" mused Julia. "I wish we knew why he speaks Chinese."

The midweek morning crowd at the Pike Place Market, named for the street which terminated in front of the main entrance, was on the lighter side, for which the sisters were grateful. The shopkeepers were scurrying about getting ready for a warm afternoon, which usually meant more shoppers. Carly wanted to see the fish being tossed, so they headed to the fish market first.

It was already abuzz with activity and cheerful voices calling to each other.

"I want to see one of those flying fish," Carly said loudly enough that the young man at the counter heard her and winked.

"Coming right up," he said, then turned and called out, "Joe, toss me a steelhead."

Julia caught the act on her cell as Joe, the fishmonger, selected a shiny whole fish, head and all, then cradled it in his arms, almost like a baby, before tossing it some twenty feet away to the clerk at the front counter.

The clerk pretended to kiss the fish on its snout, then deftly wrapped it in the craft paper. He reached out to give it to Carly, who stepped back with her hands up and shook her head.

"I'm sorry," she said. "I'm just watching."

The clerk chuckled. "I know. This fish is for that guy in the navy sweatshirt." He handed the fish to the buyer and completed the transaction, then turned back to Carly. He asked, "Do you want to know how this fish-flying stuff got started? My name's Ethan, by the way."

"Sure, Ethan. I'm Carly," she replied, suddenly aware that others in the market were moving in closer to hear him.

Ethan took a theatrical pose and told the story of how the tradition began. "Years ago, a previous owner, John Yokohama, realized he did a lot of walking in the process of selecting the fish, weighing it, packaging it, and finally delivering it to the customer at the counter. He decided to count his steps—in the days before we all had FitBits, by the way—and discovered it took at least 100 steps for each transaction." He marched in place to demonstrate. "He started throwing the fish instead, but first, he had to master the proper technique." Ethan pretended to toss a fish and acted like he had dropped it. "After many attempts, he learned to throw it in just the right way." Ethan "caught" a pretend fish and rocked it in his arms. "And he saved thousands of steps a day in the process." He bowed, and the crowd clapped.

"Do you guys have to practice a long time to get it right?" Carly asked when the clapping stopped.

"That's the first thing we learn around here. Nowadays, the customers, or spectators like you, come to expect it. So we make it fun."

"It *is* fun to watch. Thank you, Ethan."

He signed his name on a notepad and handed it to Carly. He winked and said, "Make me famous."

Carly, flustered, reddened and said, "Sure." She turned to see that Julia had recorded the whole incident as well, including the invitation to make the clerk famous. Julia pocketed her phone and noticed a lot of other people standing nearby who had also recorded the entertaining fish toss and Ethan telling the story behind it.

"I can forward the video to you if you want to post it on Facebook," said Julia.

"That'd be great." Carly turned and smiled. "Hey, I smell coffee. Can I treat you to a latte or something?" Carly grabbed Julia by the arm and started walking toward one of the several coffee vendors listed on the map.

"I'd like that."

After enjoying a vanilla latte for Carly and a London Fog for Julia, they wandered through the myriad of shops on the multiple levels of the market, which had made its debut in 1907.

Julia read from the brochure she'd picked up at the entrance to the market. "Pike Place Market is said to be the oldest continuously-running public farmer's market in the United States. It receives over ten million visitors a year, compared to the Space Needle at 1.3 million visitors. The Market is the most popular tourist attraction in Seattle and is the thirty-third most-visited tourist attraction in the world."

"That's amazing! I had no idea."

"They even have a live webcam so you can watch the fish market from home!" Julia continued. "You can watch Ethan at work from the comfort of your own chair. But don't let Rob catch you."

"Julia!"

Julia feinted to the right as Carly pretended to punch her. " Here are some more ideas from the brochure. Flower arranging? The gum wall? How about hitting a thrift shop or two? I've heard that going 'thrifting' is now a thing."

"Wasn't it always? I've found some great bargains that way."

Julia's phone rang. Beau's number lit up the screen. "Hello. Beau?"

"I need help," Beau said with panic in his voice. "Someone has kidnapped my son. We've already talked to the police, but Allison and I want you to help us. Please."

"Where are you?"

"We're at our house. The police just left. Can you come over? Carly, too, of course."

"Sure. We're at the Pike Place Market at the moment and will have to go back to the hotel to get my car. Give me an address, and I'll let you know when we're on the way."

"Thanks, Julia. We'll feel better with you in on this."

"Why on earth would someone want to kidnap Beau's son? Or want you involved?" asked Carly as Julia hailed a taxi down the street.

"There's probably something he hasn't told us, I expect," said Julia.

FIFTEEN

Julia pulled up to Beau and Allison's two-story Craftsman-style home in the Ravenna area just north of the university. The landscaping was immaculate and complemented the soft sage-colored siding with white trim. She asked her sister, "Do you remember when we came to see Aunt Jeannie and Uncle Ray when they lived in this neighborhood?"

"Gee, that was ages ago! I remember thinking there were a million trees along the streets."

"Me, too. I notice they're still here," said Julia, glancing up and down the street. "This is a gorgeous home." She took a big breath. "Are you ready for this, Carly?"

"Even though you promised me 'no detecting' this time, it looks like you'll have to eat your words." Carly sighed. "But I know you want to help find a little boy. So do I."

~

ALLISON GREETED the sisters at the door. She had obviously been crying, with telltale mascara-stained eyes and a much-used tissue in her hand. Beau joined her from the hallway, where he had been standing with his phone to his ear.

"Thank you for coming, Julia," she said, giving Julia a brief hug. "Nice to meet you, Carly. Beau told me you were here with your sister."

She led them into a handsomely appointed living room that Julia thought looked like it had been renovated recently in the trendy Scandinavian style. Thankfully, the chairs that Allison offered were more comfortable than they looked.

"Okay," said Julia once Beau had joined them, "which of you wants to tell me what happened?"

Beau looked at his wife, who sat next to him on the couch, his hand on her thigh. "Well, Allison called me a couple of hours ago. She was frantic because Benjamin, our eight-year-old son, didn't come home with his older sisters—our twelve-year-old twins—after school today. They go to a private school only three blocks from the house, and now that the girls are sixth-graders, we've been letting the kids walk back and forth by themselves unless it's really bad weather."

"And what happened today?" asked Julia. "What did your daughters say?"

"Cecily and Rylie said Benjamin's backpack was at their meeting place—a big tree just outside the playground—after school, but he wasn't there. They waited a few minutes, thinking he had run back into the building to get something. When he still hadn't shown up after another five minutes, Ariana asked a couple of the third-grade boys if they knew where he was."

"And did any of them know where he'd gone?"

"Benjamin's friend, Leo, said a fancy black car stopped right where Benjamin was standing and then some guy wearing black sweats jumped out and grabbed him. Benjamin screamed and tried to get away, but he couldn't. Then the car tore off down the street."

"Oh, no!" said Julia as she and Carly clapped their hands over their mouths.

"Leo said it happened really fast, and he couldn't remember anything about the car except it was fancy, and it had a sticker of some kind on the bumper. Of course, the girls ran home as fast as they could, and Allison called me and the police, then she raced back to the school."

"Did Leo say why he thought it was fancy?"

Allison answered, "Beau wasn't there yet, but the police asked him questions like that. It seems that the car might have been a sports car, a coupe, maybe."

"They'll probably show Leo pictures of cars to see if he can recognize one of them," said Julia.

"We already told the police everything," said Allison. "They said there wasn't much to go on yet and we should hope we'll get a call asking for ransom." She used a fresh tissue to wipe more tears from her eyes.

"Do you have any idea why Benjamin was kidnapped?" asked Julia. "Had you gotten any threatening calls, for example?" Julia looked at Allison, then Beau.

Allison had a blank look on her face as she shook her head, but Beau looked down at his hands before looking directly at Julia and saying, "Yes, in a way."

"What do you mean by that?"

"I've received a couple of emails recently that mentioned potential harm to my family if I didn't cooperate with certain requirements."

Allison looked at Beau, eyes wide. "What?"

"Meaning?" asked Julia.

"You heard Chip mention the background chatter that

appears to be coming from *Sealab Four*, right? The emails I've been getting appear to also be coming from *Sealab*."

"I will assume you've contacted the United States Navy or someone official about these emails," said Julia.

Allison moved a few inches away from her husband. "Why haven't you mentioned this to me, Beau?" she asked. "Didn't you think that would be important?"

Beau raised his hands. "I thought they were prank emails and pretty much dismissed them, until I mentioned them to Chip because of his connection to the submarine program. That's when he told me about the Jim Creek chatter. I reported them after that."

Allison sat with her arms crossed and one leg across the other, her face now angry red.

"What *were* the requirements mentioned in the emails?" asked Julia. "Do they want money?"

"I wish it were that easy. We're not rich—professors don't make that much, even at a top-ranked university—but Allison's parents are wealthy. Her dad's an investment advisor, and I hope he will help us if we ask. But that isn't what they wanted."

"But if it's not money, what is it?"

"They, and I'm not sure who 'they' are, want information from the old *Sealab* experiments."

"Why? I thought those experiments were failures."

"Maybe, in one sense of the term, but there were a lot of findings that helped us understand long-term survival in an underwater environment."

"You mean in a submarine?"

"Not exactly. I mean in another *Sealab*."

SIXTEEN

"Do you have that kind of information?" asked Julia.

"Like I said," Beau replied, "I had connections to the experts who know the most about those experiments and the conclusions that were derived from them."

"This seems like a roundabout way to go about getting that data." Julia scratched her head. "I'm sure the police officer already asked you, but did they give you instructions about delivering this information to them?"

"Not yet. They said they would call me again after I had a chance to make arrangements to get what they wanted from Scripps. That's why I was on the phone when you came to the door."

"I don't understand what Scripps has to do with this."

"It's like this. When I was in graduate school at the University of Southern California, I had the good fortune to work part-time in a research lab at Scripps Institution of Oceanography. The head of the lab had been involved in the *Sealab Three* project as a young naval engineer. The Navy officially scrapped the program in the late sixties after difficulties arose related to attempted sabotage of the air supply to the chamber and concerns about bad publicity after the USS *Pueblo* incident, when a diver died."

"I read about that online," said Julia. "I looked it up after your lecture."

"Some of the scientists involved continued to do some of the research that had been started, just not in an underwater habitat."

Julia furrowed her brows. "Are you suggesting that your earlier research working with that engineer has made you a target?"

"It's the only thing I can think of," said Beau. "The senior researchers are all gone, as in dead, and I'm the only one I know of who's still standing."

"And with unique knowledge, perhaps," said Julia. "Do you have any idea who would know that you worked there, and how they would find you?"

Carly, who had been quietly observing the conversation, jumped in. "Besides the obvious question of 'who,' why would anyone be interested in this topic?"

Beau considered his answer for a long moment before saying, "In a way, it's the same as the explanation of our human tendency to want to conquer space. As we run out of habitable land on earth, perhaps we could build underwater cities, just as some scientists propose future cities on Mars, if it turns out to be habitable after all."

Carly nodded. "Like the lost city of Atlantis, if it ever existed."

"Exactly," Beau exclaimed.

"I don't care about any of this, and neither should you," said Allison, exasperated. "I want to know how we are going to find Benjamin."

"Of course," said Julia. "I was only hoping that Beau would have some insight as to why your son was targeted. It doesn't seem likely that he would be chosen at random. Anything Beau can offer could be a clue to finding your son."

Allison turned to Beau. "Why don't you give them the information you have? Keeping it secret can't be more important than getting our Benjamin back."

"As I said, honey, I don't have direct access. It's all proprietary, classified research back at Scripps."

"Can't you get it?"

"Not directly. I was just on that call to the director and asked if they'll let me have the file, but it'll take some time, I'm afraid." He patted his wife's hand.

Allison pulled out a fresh tissue and sniffled. "The police detective, Mr. Snaza, told us to stay in touch, and if we get a ransom notice, they would be right here to help." She looked at her husband. "I never thought we would be in this situation. My precious little boy must be scared to death." She started sobbing again and leaned her head on Beau's shoulder. He put his arm around her and patted her shoulder.

"He's a little trooper, and the kidnappers have to keep him safe if they want to use him as a bargaining chip." Beau dabbed at his eyes with a handkerchief.

"You told the police all of this?" asked Julia.

Beau looked at her briefly, then averted his gaze as he answered, "Yes, of course."

Julia looked at the couple and paused, uncertain why he had called for her to come over or what he expected her to do. "Okay. Well, I'm sure the police will do their best to help you. If those photos I showed you earlier look like they might be of any help, just let me know." She rose to leave, as did Carly. "But do keep me posted."

"I'll walk you outside," said Beau. "Allison, you might want to reassure the twins. I hear some crying upstairs."

Beau went all the way to the car with his guests, then lowered his voice. "I couldn't say this in front of Allison, but there is something else that you should know."

"What would that be?"

"I got a call a couple of days ago from someone who threatened to reveal an affair I'd had if I didn't cooperate with access to the *Sealab* documents."

Julia nodded. "I'm assuming your wife doesn't know about this affair."

Beau hung his head. "I don't think so. I know it was a really stupid thing to do. And I think taking Ben is part of how they're trying to get me to help them."

"Did you tell the police about it?"

"No, not with Allison right there."

"You're going to have to come clean with it, I'm afraid," said Julia. "It's important to finding your son."

"I know. I'm so ashamed, and I don't want to lose Allison."

"You know you'll have to tell her before she finds out by some other means. The blackmailers won't be squeamish about telling her."

BACK IN THE CAR, Carly said, "I wouldn't want to have to tell Allison about an affair if I were Beau. It's bad enough that he did something so hurtful and stupid, let alone have it possibly be the reason for their son's kidnapping."

Julia nodded. "I didn't want to ask who the other party was. I have a hunch it's someone at his office, and that's why he takes his ring off there."

"I noticed he was wearing it just now. I'd worry that I would forget to put it back on before I got home."

Julia scoffed. "I'm sure that's a common worry for those who participate in such activity, but they shouldn't have started mucking around in the first place."

"Are you going to tell the police about the affair?"

Julia shrugged as she deftly moved through the street traffic back to the hotel. She was grateful that she knew routes to get around Seattle without always having to go on the freeway. "I don't think that's my prerogative, and I don't know which officer has Beau's case. So, no, I won't. Beau will have to do that."

Julia's phone rang. Detective Monroe's number flashed on her navigation screen. "Carly, will you get that, please?"

"Hi, Detective, this is Carly. Julia's driving and we're in heavy traffic, but she can hear you."

"I called to give you an update on our John Doe at the hospital."

"Do you have a name?" asked Julia.

"Not yet, but when I showed him the picture of the man you saw on the ferry, his eyes got big and he cringed and yelled, 'Traitor! Traitor!' in Chinese. The doctor had to order a sedative for him because he became so agitated."

"Did he know the other man's name?"

"If he did, he couldn't tell us. We still don't know anything useful about him."

"Darn. I was hoping he would snap out of his amnesia or something."

"Same here. The doctor did say that it's unusual for amnesia from a head injury to last longer than four or five days, so maybe we just have to wait a little longer. The hematoma under the skull is definitely smaller, but he said sometimes the brain injury itself takes longer to resolve."

"That's true. While I have you on the phone, I want to tell you about another case that might be connected."

Julia gave him a condensed version of Beau's son's abduction, recent email threats and his occupation as a nuclear engineering professor, as well as Chip Englund's connection to nuclear submarines.

"I see where you're going with this. But the man you took a photo of on the ferry simply could have happened to go to the same lecture that the John Doe went to. We have no indication that he was connected with John Doe's injuries or with the abduction. The fact that he got in a car with him could mean that they were only sharing a ride. Anyone else who had been at that lecture that night could be just as likely a suspect in your scenario."

"But you said the victim reacted to that photo. That means something, right?"

"Maybe. But the man has a head injury, and who knows what he thought when he saw that photo? Until he can tell us something we can rely on, we can't prejudge someone only because he attended the same lecture," said Monroe.

"Yes, but now an eight-year-old boy has been kidnapped, and my gut tells me there's something bigger in the background."

Detective Monroe paused before he answered, "Okay, I'll find out who the detective is on that case and talk to him. Then I can get back with you. No promises."

CHAPTER
SEVENTEEN

Julia and Carly had barely sat down to enjoy a glass of pinot grigio in the hotel lounge before returning to their room when her phone lit up again with Detective Monroe's number.

"Monroe here. Is this Ms. Fairchild?"

"I'm all ears. What do you know?"

"I talked to Detective Scott Snaza. He's assigned to that kidnapping case. He said the parents just received a call about their son, so he's meeting them at their home."

"As expected," said Julia. "Isn't that a good sign that he's still alive?"

"Generally, yes. We hope so."

"What about the submarine connection? Did you check that out?"

"Snaza is going to follow that trail because he has the Kennedy case. As of now, there isn't enough information to logically connect our John Doe and the Kennedy boy."

Julia sighed. "I just know there's something there."

"If you find something else, I'm sure you'll call me."

"Yes, sir," said Julia resignedly. She thought she heard a groan on the other end of the call.

"Who was that?" asked Carly. "You didn't put him on speaker phone."

"Oh, sorry. It was Detective Monroe. He said Beau and Allison got a call from the kidnappers, and Detective Snaza is going to meet with them at the house."

"I assume that's a good sign, as I heard you say?"

"I think it's better than no call." Julia took a big swallow of her wine. "We need to find some other link that will convince Monroe that the two cases are connected."

"What's this 'we' bit? Beau and Allison are *your* friends, not mine."

"But you do care about lost little boys, don't you?"

"Not fair, Julia. Of course I care about this little boy who is totally innocent."

"I know. So what can we come up with?" Julia picked up her almost-empty glass and drained it. "I wonder if I would be allowed to visit our John Doe at the hospital. Maybe he would recognize me from the other night."

"And if he did? Then what?"

"I have this fantasy that it would jog his memory and that he could give us a lead or something else to follow. A name. Information about the conference and why those men were there. Anything."

DETECTIVE MONROE WASN'T gung-ho about the idea but agreed to meet Julia and Carly at the hospital. He wanted to know the man's identity as much as the sisters did and didn't have a better idea, he'd said. Julia and Carly dressed in the same attire they'd worn to the ghost program, thinking it might help with his recognition of them.

The guard at the door cleared them for entry, dutifully noting their names, the date and time, and nature of their business. A Chinese-speaking nurse was already in the room. The patient was dozing when they entered—or seemed to be, as he lay softly breathing with his eyes closed.

After getting permission from the nurse, Julia touched him gently on the arm. The action caused him to open his eyes and instantly react with fright. He stared at her, then at Carly, for a moment and blinked his eyes a couple of times. "I have seen you before," he said in perfect English with an accent that was familiar but that Julia couldn't quite place. "Why do I know your face?"

Julia smiled kindly. "We saw you and your friends in downtown Seattle while waiting for a taxi last Saturday night. Do you remember?"

The man looked at her and shook his head as if puzzled. "I did not meet any friends." He snorted and crossed his arms. "Where am I now? What day is it?"

Monroe nodded to Julia to go ahead and answer. "Today is Wednesday. I am Dr. Julia Fairchild, and you are in King County Hospital, where you have been since my sister Carly—" Julia nodded at her sister, who grinned broadly, "and I found you half-dead at the arboretum."

John Doe furrowed his brows. "I don't remember any arboretum."

"That was on Sunday, and today is Wednesday. Do you remember your name?"

He scoffed. "Of course! I'm Lincoln Wellsmith the Third."

Monroe now spoke up. "I am Detective Monroe, and I need to ask you a couple of questions. First, where do you live, Mr. Wellsmith?"

"I'm from Vancouver, B.C., but I've lived in San Diego for the last fifteen years or so."

"What kind of work do you do in San Diego?" asked Monroe, his notepad in hand.

"I'm a project manager in the research lab at Scripps Institution of Oceanography. I'm one of the experts in ocean and atmospheric studies."

Julia raised an eyebrow. "Is that the same place where Dr. Beau Kennedy did some of his graduate work?"

"I don't recall that name. I'm sorry."

Julia asked, "Why did you say those men in the photo Detective Monroe showed you are traitors?"

Lincoln's face fell. "I don't know. I don't remember."

"Can you tell us why you speak fluent Chinese?" asked Julia.

"My father is a professor at the university in Vancouver, and my mother is an attorney for the city. They were too busy to take care of my two sisters and me when we were growing up, so we had a bilingual nanny who spoke Chinese. We all learned the language as youngsters. It was a fun skill to have when I was growing up." He chuckled. "Did you know there's a large Chinatown in Vancouver? Some people say it's bigger than the one in San Francisco." He smiled, then frowned. "When did I speak Chinese to you?" He looked at Julia with narrowed eyes.

"It wasn't me," said Julia. "You spoke Chinese to your nurse when you woke up for the first time after your head injury. Luckily, she understood you."

Monroe said, "I'd like to know about the three men you were with Saturday night in downtown Seattle when Dr. Fairchild and her sister first saw you."

"I don't remember anything about that."

"What about a conference at the Seattle Center? You had a

scrap of paper with the word 'nuclear' written on it when Dr. Fairchild found you. Dr. Beau Kennedy did a lecture there on nuclear submarines."

"I don't know anything about that either, officer," he said.

Monroe scrolled to the photo of the man on the ferry and showed it to Lincoln.

Lincoln studied the picture, then shook his head and said, "I don't know who that is."

Monroe and Julia looked at each other from opposite sides of the hospital bed.

"Will I be ready to be released from the hospital soon?" Lincoln asked.

"That's not up to me, but I'm not ready to release you from protective custody yet," said Monroe, "even if the doctor says you can be discharged. Someone hurt you, and they could still be out there waiting to try again."

CHAPTER

EIGHTEEN

onroe, Julia and Carly waited to talk until they were outside the building.

Julia said, "Now that you have a name, can't you enter him into the database and see if anything pops up?"

"Of course, we'll try that approach," said Monroe, "but he wasn't able to help us with a connection to the nuclear submarine issue. That might be a dead end, I'm afraid."

"And you can't hold him, because he hasn't committed a crime," said Julia, with a sigh.

"Correct. I'll call his parents in Vancouver and see if they can tell me anything. I'm still worried about his lack of memory."

"As you should be," said Julia. "In my experience, people with this kind of short-term memory loss often don't ever recover the lost bit. The brain wasn't able to record whatever was going on because of head injury occurred at a crucial time during that encryption process. Whatever he might have seen or known or done may be totally lost."

"I was afraid of that," said Monroe.

"We still have the photo of one of the other men, however, if you can track him down. Have you run his face through the traffic cameras in the city? I know you checked the area around the tour where we saw him, but he and his buddies could have been picked up before or after that evening. They had to be somewhere."

Monroe nodded grimly. "That's not a bad idea. I don't want to spend a lot of time and resources on this case, but I could assign someone to run all the tapes for Saturday and Sunday and see if anything pops up."

"I'll keep my fingers crossed," said Julia.

"Me, too," said Carly.

Monroe's phone buzzed. "Kennedy case," he said to the sisters before he stepped away out of earshot.

Julia and Carly looked at each other, eager to know what he would learn. The decibel level of the street noise around the hospital was high enough that it precluded their hearing any of Monroe's conversation.

Monroe walked the few steps back to where the sisters waited, a hard look on his face. "The kidnappers don't want money. They want information. They didn't stay on the phone long enough for us to trace the call."

"Did Beau, I mean Dr. Kennedy, say he had the information they're requesting?" asked Julia.

Monroe cocked his head. "He says he doesn't, but if he doesn't come up with something, these kidnappers might not think twice about killing his son. They're going to call again in twenty-four hours."

"Do you know who they are yet?"

"Not yet, but IT is checking in case they find any related underground chatter."

"What about investigating the attempts to hack into the military communication system at Jim Creek?" asked Julia.

Monroe arched an eyebrow. "That's way out of my league and my jurisdiction."

"It might be the connection you're looking for if Dr. Kennedy's lecture on nuclear submarines and his previous work on *Sealab* are the trigger for kidnapping little Ben."

"Thank you. I'll stay in touch."

"I FEEL SO HELPLESS," said Julia once they were back in the car. "I'm beginning to wish we'd never seen Lincoln and those other three men."

"The trouble didn't start until we found him at the arboretum," said Carly. "And then went to the Science Center."

"I suppose," said Julia. "But we can't go backward and forget what we saw."

"Actually, we can. The police are doing the investigations, not us."

"But what about the cyber hacking attempt and the *Sealab* links?"

"What about them? The police are taking care of the kidnapping case. There's nothing you and I can do. And there's still a lot of Seattle to see if you will remember that we are *on vacation.*"

Julia turned and smiled at her sister. "You're right. Let's have a nice dinner somewhere tonight and figure out what we'll do tomorrow."

"You're starting to talk like a normal person. Finally." Carly set the GPS and said, "We're going to Duke's Seafood and Chowder on Fairview next to Lake Union. I'm hungry for seafood."

~

"This is a wonderful place for dinner," said Julia. "You know how much I love being near the water. Good choice, sis."

"Isn't it funny that we both love seafood even though we were raised on a farm and had all the beef and chicken we wanted?"

"Yes, but Grandpa T. fished, and we had a lot of steelhead and salmon, as well as sturgeon. Remember how Daddy used to smoke fish in the smokehouse by the chicken coop?"

"Of course. The burning barrel was next to it, and I got into a lot of trouble the time I was playing 'fairy' with a stick and almost started the chicken coop on fire."

"I think you were only four or five years old at the time. I know Mom wanted to punish you, but Dad didn't believe in spanking, fortunately for you." Julia smiled kindly at her sister.

"The look he gave me was enough to set me straight."

"I got that look a few times growing up, too." Julia took a bite of her entrée, Dungeness crab served with a light Hollandaise sauce. "This crab is delicious," said Julia. "The roasted asparagus is perfect, and this bread is like homemade. How are those prawns?"

"I can't resist ordering anything that's sautéed in garlic butter." Carly wiped the butter from her chin and hands as she said, "They taste even better when I get to eat them with my fingers."

"I'm getting spoiled. I'm not going to want to cook when I get home."

"I *never* want to cook, but I don't think Rob will let me get away with that."

The sisters giggled and chatted about a mutual fantasy of having live-in cooks and maids and living a life of doing whatever they wanted while someone else took care of running the household.

"I have it easier than you for now," said Julia, "because

there's only my dog and me. And Trixie is pretty easy to please."

Carly raised her glass of pinot grigio to Julia's glass of viognier. "Someday, you'll meet that Prince Charming."

"Probably not in Parkview," Julia said wistfully.

NINETEEN

"We haven't decided what to do tomorrow," said Carly once they were back in their comfortable room. She and Julia stood on their balcony enjoying a second glass of wine as they watched the harbor traffic go by. The sun had set long ago, and the stars and moon shone against the inky-black sky to the west. Even the city lights of Seattle couldn't fully drown out the brightest stars.

"Want to try the Ferris wheel down at the pier? It looks massive. I love that feeling that I get just as the wheel starts back down from the top, and you think you're going to fall off the edge of the world." Julia sighed as her memory recreated that sensation.

"Sure, and maybe we can take that harbor ride from Pier 55. It says in this brochure that it's a one-hour narrated cruise. We'll see the Seattle skyline, the shipping port, and 'sweeping views of the Olympic Mountains.'"

"We can see the Olympic Mountains from right here," said Julia, "if you haven't noticed."

"That's not the same as seeing them from the water."

"True. Sounds fine to me. Does one o'clock sound okay to you?"

"Sure. You can make the reservations," said Carly. "You still owe me from being stranded in the powerboat when we went to Virgin Gorda."

"How many times will I have to pay you back, anyway?" Julia asked. "Isn't treating you to a vacation and fancy meals enough?"

"Depends on how many times you put me in perilous situations."

"So far this week, I've done okay. Not one time!"

Carly sniggered. "There's still time. Don't count those chickens too soon."

As if on cue, Julia's phone buzzed. Chip Englund's number popped up. Julia frowned and said to Carly, "I wonder what Chip could want." She shrugged and said, "Hi. This is Julia."

"Thank you for answering. I wasn't sure if you would take my call, being as you hardly know me."

"I might not have, except I entered your contact info earlier. What's going on?"

"Beau just called to tell me about the kidnapping. He's really scared."

"Which is understandable," Julia said.

"Did he tell you anything about what the kidnappers want?"

"A little, but I didn't really understand why it would be so important. It sounded like old material to me." Julia looked at Carly with a raised eyebrow.

"Didn't he tell you about his recent research?"

"No, not in so many words."

"Oh, I thought he may have told you something more about that. Did you get to meet his grad student, Laci Lia?"

"He introduced her to us when we met him at his office. Why?"

"He probably didn't tell you he had been having an affair with her. And he's afraid his wife will find out."

There was a moment of silence until Chip said, "Beau may hate me for telling you this, but it may be the only way we can help."

"Just tell me already," said Julia.

"There was another grad student at Scripps when Beau was there. They were working on different aspects of the same project."

"He said they were all dead and gone. What gives?"

"Technically, he's correct. All the *senior* investigators are gone, but not this guy."

"How do you know?"

"His name was on the list I saw from the nuclear energy conference."

"Are you saying Beau lied about not knowing any of them?"

Chip cleared his throat. "In his field of work, you might understand that there's a finite number of experts. And they each tend to have a particular area of focus for their research. They're also a bit egotistic and jealously guard their findings."

"I can see that," said Julia. "I read a book recently about gene editing. Part of the story involved the competition among scientific teams to develop a workable solution, with a fortune at stake for the winners."

"Yes, money usually matters when groundbreaking science is involved."

"I don't understand." Julia shrugged a shoulder, which Chip couldn't see over the phone. "What would be groundbreaking about the *Sealab* research?"

"From what I understand, the research team that Beau worked with discovered ways to solve the heat-cold transfer issues underwater, as well as the oxygen system. You may remember from your reading that getting oxygen to the bathysphere 200 feet below sea level was quite the challenge."

"So?"

"What if that's the information that someone wants so they can develop a new underwater development?"

"Sounds a little too much like science fiction to me," said Julia. "I mean, is that really feasible? And what does it have to do with the name on the list?"

"I'm not certain, but I think he might be working for the Chinese government. Maybe in their military, which is notoriously corrupt. And he's Laci Lia Ling's uncle."

"Are you suggesting that Beau might be somehow connected to all this through Laci Lia?"

"Wouldn't you think the same thing?"

After they hung up, Julia filled Carly in on the half of the conversation she couldn't hear. "I'm not sure if either Chip *or* Beau is telling me the whole truth. I prefer to believe it's Beau, but that could be just because I've known him longer."

"Why would Chip call *you*? What could you possibly do to help?" Carly went back to reading her novel.

"It felt like he was trying to find out if I knew anything about Beau's research, which, of course, I don't. Or maybe to throw doubt on Beau."

"As in fishing for information?"

"Yeah, like that. I feel bad for Beau, but I'm at a loss to help him. And I'm not eager to jump in when I know he's had an affair."

"It would be easier if the kidnapper only wanted money."

"Yes, except Allison might not go along with it once she knows about Beau's affair."

"I'm sure all she cares about right now is getting her little boy back," said Carly. "I imagine she'll take care of Beau later.

Now let's get some sleep before another busy day of sight-seeing tomorrow."

Julia nodded, and they started to prepare for bed. But she couldn't help but think Allison would be worried over her son's safety and ignorant of what could be behind her little boy's kidnapping. For Allison, Julia knew there would be little sleep tonight.

CHAPTER

TWENTY

The sun was glorious the next morning. The forecast for the afternoon boat ride was promising, with low, scattered clouds, a temperature of sixty-five, and no rain.

After a brisk walk along the seaboard to Anthony's and back to the hotel, Julia was looking forward to a quiet morning with her book, *Splintered Silence,* by Susan Furlong. Her sister already had her nose in the Louise Penny novel she'd started earlier.

Julia's eyes widened when she saw Beau's name show up on her cell. Carly shot her a glance. "Who is it?"

"Hi, Beau. What's going on?" she asked, concerned she may hear bad news about Benjamin.

"I thought you'd want to know that we were able to get Ben back."

"Oh, that's wonderful news! I'm sure you and Allison are thrilled beyond imagination. How did that come about?" Julia's antennae twitched.

"Fortunately, they settled for money, and Allison's dad was willing to cover us for it."

"Why the change?"

"I convinced them I couldn't get the data from the Navy or Scripps, and they finally agreed to release Ben for a million dollars."

"That's a relief. Is Ben okay after his ordeal? That had to have been frightening for him."

"He's okay. He's a little trooper." Beau chuckled. "All he wanted when he got home was moose crunch ice cream."

"Good choice. That's one of my favorites."

"Mine, too. Anyway, thank you for trying to help. Let's stay in touch."

"Okay. Bye, Beau."

Julia looked at the phone for a moment after ending the call and shook her head. "That was strange."

"What's strange?"

"Beau said the kidnappers settled for money after all, and everything is okay now."

"That doesn't sound like what usually happens. What happened to wanting that research data?"

Julia shrugged. "He must have convinced them somehow that he didn't have it and couldn't get the material after all. And according to Chip, Beau doesn't have direct access to it."

"That doesn't make sense to me. Why would they settle so quickly? Oh well. At least we can forget about that and act like normal tourists again," said Carly.

"Except for Lincoln."

"Who's Lincoln?" Carly scowled. "Oh, yeah. The arboretum guy who now has a name, and he's not your problem either anymore."

. . .

RAIN JACKETS—JUST in case, despite the favorable forecast—and cameras in hand, Julia and Carly walked to Pier 55 to start their cruise of the harbor along Seattle's waterfront.

"I wonder if our guy has been discharged from the hospital yet," said Julia as they strolled down the sidewalk with the water to their right.

Carly shrugged. "He certainly seemed to be getting better, last we heard."

"And he has family who can take care of him if he needs it, so that's good."

"Why are you worried about him? He's fine. Problem solved." Carly pointed at the Ferris wheel. "We still need to ride that monster. What about after the boat tour?"

"Great idea. I wonder what kind of work Lincoln does in San Diego."

"Julia…"

A group of people gathered around the gate for the cruise, which was to start at one twenty-five p.m. About thirty people stood in line to buy tickets. Some of them apparently hoped to squeeze onto the boat that was leaving in a few minutes despite the ticket seller telling them it was already full.

"It's a good thing we did online reservations," said Julia. "This great weather is probably the reason there's such a crowd on a weekday."

"Yeah, it's not spring break or any kind of holiday."

The sisters managed to score port-side positions along the rail of the main deck. Julia made a quick trip to the bar for a couple of glasses of prosecco to enjoy.

"It feels like we should be celebrating something, but I can't think of what it might be," said Julia.

"Let's see. How about the fact that we haven't spent the whole week chasing criminals?"

"That's good. And our John Doe has a name."

"And Ben has been released from the kidnappers."

"All good reasons," said Julia. "Cheers!"

THE NARRATION of the tour began, interrupting the conversation. Julia and Carly listened to the stories of the history and development of Seattle over the previous 150 years as the two-level boat motored past the downtown area, the southern waterfront, out to Alki Point, across the inner harbor toward Blake Island, and finally back around Elliott Bay to the starting point at the pier.

The sun sparkled on the calmer-than-usual water, and the breeze was pleasantly mild instead of bone-chillingly cold.

"The wind typically picks up later in the day around here," said a man who stood at the rail next to Julia. "The local sailing clubs take advantage of that. It allows them to race in the evenings after work on the weekdays once the days get long enough."

"Are you one of those sailors?" asked Julia.

"I can't imagine how you guessed," he said, winking at her. "Too bad you're not here a month later. All summer long, the city of Seattle sponsors Thursday night sailboat racing along the waterfront. It brings out the locals as well as the visitors along the piers. The racers participate because they love to race any chance they get, plus the whole crew gets free food, beer and wine afterward. There are all kinds of vendors competing for the chance to be one of the sponsors. You wouldn't believe the prizes that the sailors might win just for showing up."

"So, it's not a race where you have first-, second- and third-place winners?"

"No," he said, shaking his head. "It's purely for fun. Any boat that participates has its name placed in the bucket, and if that boat's name is drawn, the crew wins whatever the prize is.

Some are small, like baseball hats or a five-dollar Starbucks gift card. One time I won the big prize with a duffle bag, a couple of T-shirts and a gift card for a hundred and fifty dollars at a local boat supply place." He grinned. "I might have come in last that week, but winning isn't everything out on the water."

"That does sound like fun," said Carly.

"Maybe we should make a return trip this summer," said Julia.

The captain announced the imminent docking of the cruise boat, with the usual reminder that everyone should check to be sure they had all their belongings, including children they had brought along. Julia chuckled as one guest nearby said she was tempted to leave one of hers aboard but didn't want the state social worker at her door accusing her of abandonment.

"THAT WAS REALLY FUN," said Carly. "I might be getting over my fear of being in a boat. At least as long as you're not driving."

Julia poked her in the ribs. "You need to be nice. Or you could have a long walk back home from Seattle."

The sisters laughed as they disembarked the boat. "Should we ride the Ferris wheel now or wait till dark?" asked Julia.

"Definitely let's wait till it's dark. I want to see the lights of the city from the top of it."

"Okay by me. Let's stop and have a glass of iced tea at one of these sidewalk cafes before we go back to the hotel. I'm not ready to be done yet."

Julia and Carly entered Ivar's and sat at a high-top table overlooking the water. They watched as seagulls fought over clams. One seagull would drop a clam from about ten feet in the air onto the concrete surface, breaking the shell. Often another seagull would swoop in to claim it before the first seagull was able to recover its meal. They screeched noisily at each other while the process repeated itself again and again.

Julia sat with her elbows on the table, deep in thought. "I don't understand what happened with Beau's kidnapping situation. It just doesn't make sense that the kidnappers would settle for a mere million dollars if the information Beau had access to were truly worth a lot more than that."

"Maybe they found another way to get to it. Chip said there was another researcher in the group that Beau forgot to mention to you."

"I suppose that's a possibility." Julia sighed. "My gut tells me there's something wrong with the story. But what?"

"I assume that's a rhetorical question, because I'm letting the police take care of it." Carly glared at her sister. "And so are you."

Julia made a face at her, then started giggling as Carly returned the favor. They walked arm in arm back to the hotel, enjoying the warmth of the sun. It felt almost like summer.

They walked into the hotel lobby and paused when they saw Detective Monroe standing at the receptionist's desk. He turned his head when he heard the door open. When he saw it was Julia and Carly, he thanked the desk clerk for her help and met the sisters halfway across the room.

"Hello, Ms. Fairchild, Ms. Pedersen. I was hoping to catch you."

"Has something happened?" asked Julia.

"Kind of. Mr. Wellsmith seems to have recaptured more memory and wants to talk to you. He won't tell me whatever it is that he's remembered, so I came down here to see if you're available to go with me to the hospital. He's about to be discharged but agreed to wait for you if I could find you."

CHAPTER

TWENTY-ONE

Lincoln Wellsmith III was dressed in street clothes and sitting in a chair in his room when the trio arrived. He rose as they entered and asked that Monroe close the door behind him.

"Hi, Mr. Wellsmith," said Julia. "The detective tells me that you have something to share."

"Please call me Lincoln," he said, smiling, "and have a seat. It finally came back to me about what happened last Saturday night. I was with three men, one of whom I know from my work at Scripps in San Diego." He pointed to the chair next to where he was seated.

"Is he the one in the picture that I took on the ferry?" Julia quickly pulled up the photo and showed it to Lincoln.

"Yes. His name is Sheldon Stanley. I met him when I was working in San Diego. He had finished his degree in journalism and was working for the local newspaper. I had been compiling data from the research done during the early years after the third *Sealab* project was scrapped. Now and then, he'd ask about my work when we met for drinks. I understand you know a little about the project. Is that correct?"

Julia and Carly nodded.

Julia asked, "Why would you be bothering with that old data?"

"One of the senior researchers had stumbled onto a couple of memos from about fifteen years ago that mentioned a fourth *Sealab* experiment, which never happened as far as I know. I decided to do some digging and found some references to the dolphin and sea lion training program, which, as you might know, is based in San Diego."

"Yes, we heard about it from one of my friends," said Julia. "He told us about how they patrol the coastline up at Bangor, one of the submarine bases here in Washington."

"Well, Sheldon left San Diego a couple of years later to do bigger and better things. I didn't know what he was doing or where he was working, but a month ago, he contacted me and said he would be at the nuclear energy conference at the Seattle Center, and would I meet him there. He knew I would likely be planning to attend because it's one of the conferences I usually go to. There's always a slate of excellent speakers, and I usually learn something new or intriguing."

"So that's why you were here. You know my sister and I saw you and your three companions after we had been on the 'Spooked in Seattle' tour, right?"

He nodded. "I remember your face vividly. Maybe because you resemble my sister, with your dark hair and your kind face. Anyway, Sheldon and the other two men were forcing me to get into a car when I saw you. Sheldon started talking about a project involving the Chinese government and implied I might somehow be connected to it, which frightened me. I thought it might be because he knows I speak Chinese. I jumped out of the car at a stoplight before I learned any more. I ran into a bar and hid in the men's room for a while until I thought they had gone."

"Did they come looking for you? Or did they keep going?" asked Julia.

"I thought they had continued driving without me because when I came out of the bar about ten minutes later and looked up and down the street, I didn't see any of them or the car Sheldon had been driving. So I called Uber for a ride and waited just outside the door. When I stepped out of the doorway to look for the Uber driver's silver Prius, I heard someone behind me. That's when I was clunked from behind."

"Do you think it was Sheldon or his men?"

"I turned just in time to see a face. It wasn't Sheldon or anyone I knew. But I don't know what happened from the moment I was struck from behind until I woke up at the hospital. That memory is totally lost."

"That's a common occurrence with head injuries," said Julia. "If the brain isn't awake, it can't process or store any new information. It's called post-traumatic amnesia. The memory's just not there because a brain that's asleep can't process any information. But memory preceding the traumatic brain injury will usually be retained and often recovered once the brain has healed—at least, in a mild to moderate injury."

"Does that mean I might never remember what happened after I was hit, and I should stop trying?" Lincoln looked at Julia with a furrowed brow.

"Basically, yes. It might drive you nuts trying to recall something that isn't there to begin with. You might have been the victim of a robbery and left at the arboretum to make it harder to identify your assailant. That would explain why you didn't have a phone or a wallet on you."

"Okay. One more thing. I thought Sheldon might have said

the word 'conspiracy' just before I jumped out of the car. I thought he meant me."

"Do you think that's why you called him a traitor when you saw his picture?"

"It's the only thing that comes to mind. I wish I could remember if he said anything more. And if I said anything."

"What about the other two men?" asked Detective Monroe. "Is there anything you can recall?"

Lincoln shook his head. "I wish I could. I can only guess that they were partners or friends of Sheldon's. I didn't know them, and I don't remember any names at all."

Julia said to Monroe, "I just thought of something. That list you got from Dr. Kennedy's grad student, Laci Lia, might contain the names. Is it on your cell phone?"

Monroe quickly pulled up the list and showed it to Lincoln, who pointed out Sheldon's name but didn't recognize any of the others.

Julia asked, "Earlier, you said you did not recall Dr. Kennedy, but do you now? Did you work on the *Sealab* project at about the time?"

"Yes, I recall him, but we were not friends, only coworkers in passing."

"Does Beau know Sheldon? Was he there in the same timeframe?"

"Sometimes Beau was with us when we had drinks. So, yes, he knew him."

"I can do a trace on Sheldon Stanley and see if anything pops up," said Monroe. "Thank you, Mr. Wellsmith."

Julia handed Lincoln her business card. "If you remember anything else, you can call me, if it's okay with Detective Monroe." She glanced at the detective, who nodded in return.

Having said their goodbyes and thank yous, they stepped

into the hall, where they found a young woman leaning against the wall, waiting.

"Are you here to see Mr. Wellsmith?" asked Monroe.

"Yes, I'm his sister Perdita." She offered her hand. Julia noted that she had dark hair in a similar hairstyle as her own.

"I'm Detective Monroe with the Seattle Police Department," he said as he returned the handshake. "This is Dr. Julia Fairchild and her sister Carly Pedersen." He indicated each as he said her name. "They found your brother at the arboretum. Maybe even saved his life." He managed a tiny smile.

"Thank you, Dr. Fairchild and Miss Pedersen," she said as they exchanged greetings. "I understand from the doctor this morning that he's going to be okay except possibly for some residual memory loss. He's agreed to stay with my family and me for a few days here in Seattle before going back to San Diego."

"Good plan," said Julia.

"We're still investigating the incident and hope to find his attackers," said Monroe. "We wish you well."

Once they were in the elevator and away from any stray ears, Julia asked, "Will you let me know if anything comes of your investigation into Mr. Stanley? I know it's not really any of my business, but I'd like to know the rest of the story if there is one."

"I'll give you a call." He tipped his hat. "I hope you two enjoy the remainder of your week."

BACK AT THE HOTEL AGAIN, Julia checked her email while Carly sent a message to her husband, Rob.

"What a surprise," said Julia. "Here's a short note from Josh. He says he's thinking of me and hopes we're enjoying

Seattle. And he's figuring out the subway system. He's only gotten on the wrong train twice this week so far." She chuckled. "I remember when we were headed the wrong direction one time, and some kind people told us how to go back the right way without having to pay a second fare."

"Subways still scare me. I prefer to be able to look out a window and see where I'm going."

"Me too." Julia sent a quick note in response. She'd felt disappointed that he hadn't joined her on this trip—worried, to be honest, whether it indicated a problem with their relationship. Hearing from him now made her smile.

"I'm worried that Lincoln could still be in danger," she said when she was done.

"Not. Your. Problem." Carly's fingers flew as she composed her own, much longer, note.

"I know, but I worry about him. If Sheldon and his companions were able to track Lincoln down once, they could probably do it again."

"He'll be with his sister and probably will be safe enough," said Carly. "Hopefully, they don't have her contact information."

"I wonder what kind of project Sheldon would be working on with the Chinese government. He clearly isn't Chinese himself, and those other thugs didn't look Asian."

"Doesn't it almost always boil down to money? I can think of a few headlines in the past that were all about making big money illegally."

"I suppose that's a possibility. I wonder if Beau knows this Sheldon guy. I'm going to call him."

"And if he says he does?"

"For one thing, it'll prove that he lied when he said he didn't know any of the names on that list."

TWENTY-TWO

"Yeah, I vaguely remember Sheldon and his wife," said Beau. "She was one of those whiz-kid, super-smart women from Taiwan. She was beautiful, too. Her name was something like Wenming, but she went by 'Wendy.' It was easier for the rest of us to pronounce."

Julia visualized Beau drooling over this Wendy. "Do you know anything about them now? Like where he works or lives?"

"Gee, I haven't thought about him in at least five years. Why?"

"It was one of the names on that list that Laci Lia sent to the detective. It's the only name Detective Monroe couldn't trace." Julia crossed her fingers behind her back even though Beau couldn't see them.

"Oh. I hadn't noticed it when I saw the list, but I wasn't looking very closely."

Julia felt her antennae twitch. *Was he lying about not recognizing that name? And if so, why?*

"How's your little boy doing? Has he gone back to school?"

"Ben's fine. He's acting like nothing happened, for which I'm glad."

"Please give him a little extra moose crunch ice cream for me."

"Sure thing," said Beau. "Thanks for checking."

After they disconnected, Julia held the phone in her hand for a moment as if it were a lie detector apparatus. "I wonder why Beau lied about Sheldon."

"What do you mean? Remember, I can only hear what *you* say when you're on the phone."

"I'm not sure, but I think he knows Sheldon better than he says he does. He said he didn't recognize the name on the list and earlier denied recognizing him in the photo from the ferry."

"I noticed you didn't tell Beau that some of Lincoln's memory came back."

"Some sixth sense told me not to reveal that bit of information to Beau just yet. Maybe not even to Chip."

"Perhaps Monroe should check into Beau's background, as long as he's researching that Sheldon guy," said Carly.

Julia called Monroe, reached his voice mail, and left a brief message suggesting such a check.

"WHAT WOULD Dad have said if he could have experienced this Ferris wheel ride?" Carly held up her glass of wine in a salute. They were approaching the highest point of the monster-sized wheel. "Being able to enjoy a drink and the city views at the same time is amazing."

"He was always a good sport about going on the rides at the fair with us. I don't know if he actually liked the Hammerhead, but you younger kids wouldn't go with me, so he did. What a guy." Julia raised her glass and took a swallow at the very top of the wheel's revolution. "Here's to Dad." The sisters were quiet for a few moments, mesmerized by the night lights of the city and the harbor. A faint tinge of pink lingered behind the Olympic Mountains. It gave a mystical aura to the western horizon.

"This ride is pretty spectacular," said Julia. "I didn't realize these cabs were enclosed, but it makes sense, with Seattle weather being so unpredictable."

"Plus, it makes it possible to take a ride year-round," said Carly. "Clever planning on someone's part."

"Indeed." Julia surveyed the eastern horizon toward the Cascade Mountains as the wheel began its descent. "Carly, what did you think of Lincoln's comments about those memos he mentioned? He's the third person this week to refer to those *Sealab* experiments."

"Didn't he also say something about the Chinese government?" asked Carly.

"Yes. It makes me wonder about Beau," said Julia. "He mentioned getting emails from a source tied to *Sealab Four*. And now Lincoln mentioned it. There's got to be something to it."

"Chip mentioned the cyber hackers also being tied to *Sealab*."

"I wonder what's at the bottom of this. It's like trying to work a jigsaw puzzle that includes pieces that don't fit the picture on the box. And left out the ones that are supposed to be there."

"Thankfully, we don't have to figure it out. Drink your wine before the ride is done, Julia."

• • •

"WHAT A BEAUTIFUL EVENING for walking back to the hotel," said Julia. "No wind, the moon is up, and the temperature is perfect."

"What do you think of doing the laser show tomorrow night? We talked about it earlier, but I think our plan got shanghaied that evening," said Carly.

"Sounds good. It'll be a fun way to end our week in the big city."

"My turn to get the door," said Carly as they approached the hotel. She scurried to open it before Julia did. They laughed, having reached for the handle at the same time. They stepped into the lobby and went a few more steps before they stopped laughing and slowed their walking. Sheldon Stanley stood next to the cookie bar.

Julia and Carly took several more steps toward the elevator.

"You can stop walking and turn around. We're all going back outside," said Sheldon. He had his right hand in his jacket pocket.

Julia didn't see a desk clerk. The lobby was empty of other guests. She suspected Sheldon had a gun in his hand. She considered ignoring his command and walking to the reservation desk but figured Sheldon wouldn't hesitate to do something to stop her. She looked at Carly, whose eyes were as big as they could be and said, "Sure. We can talk outside."

As soon as they exited the building, two men emerged from the darkness and grabbed their arms. "Don't scream," Sheldon admonished. "It makes my friends jumpy, and they might accidentally shoot you. Let's walk over to the limousine at the curb."

Julia shivered despite being warm. She tried to communicate reassurance via ESP to her sister while frantically trying to recall the instructions she'd learned at work about getting away from an attacker. Unfortunately, none of the lessons had addressed a situation with three bad guys, at least one of whom seemed to have a gun.

The man gripping Julia's right arm with his left hand reached out to open the door of the limo. He pushed her inside and slid into the seat across from her. The other thug did the same with Carly on the opposite side. Sheldon entered the limo's back seat as well, took a seat next to thug number one, and sat facing Julia and Carly. He told the driver to leave the curb and start driving.

"So you're Beau's little friends," Sheldon said with a sneer.

"Friends from college. Nothing more," said Julia.

"That's not what he tells me. He said you've been playing detective."

Julia shrugged. "I don't know what he would mean by that. We're here on vacation and have been playing tourist all week."

"Why were you at the nuclear conference on Monday?"

"We saw the poster on the kiosk when we had lunch at the Space Needle. My sister thought she could learn something to take back to her company to lower their energy bills."

Sheldon narrowed his eyes at Carly. "Is that true?"

She nodded her head vigorously. "ESCO is a major pulp and paper company with huge electricity bills. Nuclear energy is the way to go."

"Hm. My friend Lincoln was discharged from the hospital today. Did you know that?"

"No, sir," said Julia. "We don't know anyone named Lincoln—unless you mean President Abe Lincoln, and he's dead."

"Quick with your tongue, aren't you?"

"Extemporaneous speaking and impromptu were my specialties in high school debate," said Julia, more bravely than she felt. "That was a lot of years ago, however."

"What do you know about *Sealab*?"

"Only what Dr. Kennedy mentioned in his talk on nuclear submarines. Sounded like ancient history to me."

Julia had been paying attention to where the limo driver was going as Sheldon played his version of twenty questions. They had driven south down Alaskan Way, then turned east onto Spring Street, traveling away from the harbor. She had worried he would follow the street all the way onto I-5, but the driver turned north again and cruised up Fourth Avenue instead, several blocks east of the harbor.

"You know I can find you if you do anything stupid, Dr. Fairchild," Sheldon snarled.

Julia noticed the limo turning left down Clay Street, which ended near their hotel. "I have clinic patients waiting to see me on Monday. I wouldn't want to disappoint them."

"Keep your nose out of business that doesn't concern you." Sheldon indicated to the driver to pull up in front of the Edgewater once they were back on Alaskan Way.

Once the car stopped and the thugs got out of their way, Julia and Carly got out of the limousine as quickly as they could. Julia managed to step heavily on the instep of thug number one's foot as he stood aside to let her out. "Oh! Excuse me. I'm so sorry." She grabbed Carly's hand once they were both outside the limo, made one backward glance at the car's license plate, and then ran across the parking lot to the door.

TWENTY-THREE

"That was not my idea of fun," said Carly once they were safely inside the lobby.

"That meeting wasn't on my agenda for the evening, but it certainly raises my suspicion about what Beau and Sheldon may be doing in the background."

"It raises my fear level, not my curiosity." Carly pressed the elevator button. "Let's go back to our room and call the detective. He'll want to know about this."

"What does *Sealab* have to do with all this, I wonder?" said Julia.

"I don't think I want to know," said Carly.

"And what does Chip have to do with it?"

"Not my problem."

"There has to be some connection that makes sense," said Julia. "I wish Lincoln could remember more of what happened that night."

"And I wish we had never met Sheldon," said Carly as she opened the door to their room. She entered the room slowly and peeked into the bedroom and bathroom, just in case.

"Where's the rest of that bottle of wine? I need something. My hands are still shaking."

Julia obligingly poured the wine and dropped into one of the two comfortable chairs. She pressed Detective Monroe's number and was rewarded with an immediate, "Yes, Dr. Fairchild?"

Julia gave him a brief rundown of their short but unsettling kidnapping session with Sheldon. "I'm beginning to think that it wasn't an accident that Sheldon and his buddies attended Beau's lecture. There's got to be some kind of fishy connection between Beau and Chip—and probably Lincoln, too."

"Do you remember anything else that Mr. Stanley said or asked?" Julia pictured Monroe writing down notes in his ever-handy notepad unless he was dismissing what she told him.

"He mostly asked if I knew Lincoln and anything about *Sealab*. And he knew that I had been friends with Beau."

"Did he threaten you?"

"No, but he told me to mind my own business."

"That was probably for your own safety," said Monroe. "I would ask that you do the same. We can handle this. Thank you for calling. Good night, Dr. Fairchild."

Julia made a face at her phone as she set it down.

"Why the look?" asked Carly.

"Monroe basically told me to stay out of the investigation."

"I've told you the same thing, sis. It's out of your league."

"Yeah, yeah, yeah. But there are still unanswered questions, like why was Lincoln assaulted? What is it that he refused to do?"

Carly took a couple of swallows of her wine. "What if Lincoln's injuries were part of a staged set-up of some kind? I mean, why didn't they just kill him instead of whacking him and leaving him where he could be found? If it was Sheldon's thugs, that is."

"Hm. If they really thought he was a risk or liability to whatever they were trying to do, I wouldn't think they would want him alive. He could talk."

"Do you suppose he just pretended to have amnesia? I would think a person could easily fake it."

"But why would he fake it?" Julia's thoughts wandered for a moment. "Maybe his attacker intended to kill him and didn't expect him to survive. So when we found him and saved his life, whoever wanted him dead had to go to a different plan."

"The old Plan B like in the movies," said Carly, giggling.

Julia sat up straighter in her chair. "Sheldon said someone was following us. Maybe it's whoever whacked Lincoln."

"We still don't know who that was."

Julia sat back in her chair, legs tucked under her. "Beau, Chip and Lincoln have all mentioned the *Sealab* experiments. China and the United States both have nuclear submarine fleets which could theoretically be considered mobile versions of those early *Sealab* stations."

"Huh? I don't understand."

"From the little bit of research I did, it seems that those underwater units were testing survivability underwater without having to be in a submarine. Submarines have been around since before World War Two, so why would anyone be interested in something like a *Sealab*? They're stationary and can't go anywhere. What would they be good for? And why does anybody care now?"

"Just thinking of the logistics of getting oxygen to something like that underwater is mind-boggling," said Carly.

"Maybe the interest isn't in the *Sealab* itself, but in some specific aspect of the research." Julia sat sideways in her chair and let her legs dangle over the side of the arm. "Lincoln said Beau did some of that ongoing work when he was in grad school." She sighed as she reached for her wine. "I wish I had asked more questions about that."

"He probably wouldn't have told you, if he's in on this whole scheme."

Julia sipped her wine. "I just hope he isn't, and that he's an innocent bystander like we are."

"Do you think Beau might be doing some of that research now in his lab at the university?" Carly poured a little more wine for her sister and herself. "Maybe that's what the kidnappers really want, not the old stuff."

"That's actually a good thought. And it makes more sense than old material from nearly sixty years ago." Julia sat up. "What if Laci Lia has something to do with all this?"

"What are you thinking?"

"Chip mentioned that there was a Chinese student working with Beau at the Scripps Lab. And that he was Laci Lia's uncle."

"Didn't he also say he thought the guy worked for the Chinese government now?"

"Yes." Julia stood up and started pacing the room. "We need to talk to Beau and probably Laci Lia, too."

"Why you and me and not Detective Monroe?"

"Because we know about both sides of this situation."

"What do you mean by that?"

"The way I see it, we saw Sheldon and his men with Lincoln, then found Lincoln at the arboretum. That's the case Monroe knows."

Carly nodded slowly.

"And we got sucked into the kidnapping side with Beau and Allison, which is in the hands of Detective Snaza, not Monroe."

"Oh, I get it now," said Carly. "You're thinking that because we are familiar with both cases, we should get even more involved." She shook her head and crossed her arms.

"That's not exactly how I was looking at it. We simply have a more complete picture than either detective."

"Julia, there really isn't anything to solve at this point. Beau's little boy has been returned, Lincoln is identified and safe with his sister, and I don't give a hang about the references to *Sealab*."

"When you put it like that, it does seem a little silly to spend any more energy on it."

"Now you're coming to your senses," said Carly.

"Except there's still the matter of Sheldon and his thugs, and why did they take us for that little ride?"

"You know, we only have one more day in Seattle. I'd like to enjoy it and not worry about anything else. Can we do that?"

"You're right. It's not our problem. We'll do that laser light show tomorrow night and head home Saturday."

"Now you're talking."

"But it wouldn't hurt to send this license plate number to Monroe."

TWENTY-FOUR

"Yes, I can run the plate number for you, Dr. Fairchild, but the likelihood of coming up with anything useful is slim," said Detective Monroe. "I would put money on it being a rental, which could be under anybody's name." Julia thought she could hear sounds of traffic in the background.

"Thank you, sir. We were scared to death when Sheldon and his pals took us for a ride, and I didn't think of that."

"You should choose your friends more carefully," he said with an edge to his voice.

"Yes, Sir. Carly and I are leaving Seattle Saturday morning to go home, where the natives are much friendlier."

"Be careful until then, please. Goodbye."

Julia grimaced as she ended the call. "I can't tell if he's sad or glad to see us go."

"Probably more glad that nobody got killed because of us," said Carly. She was absorbed in her book and only half-listened.

"There's still something going on with Beau and Sheldon, and maybe Chip, but I sure can't figure it out."

"Not your problem, remember?"

Julia made a face at her sister, even though Carly wasn't looking at her. She picked up her mystery and tried to recall what had happened the previous few pages. She sighed and put the book aside. She settled back in her chair as if inspiration would suddenly strike. Her phone rang instead.

"Who is it?" asked Carly.

Julia grimaced at her phone. "Chip. I wonder what he wants this time. Hello, Chip. How can I help you?"

"Hey. I just got a call from Allison, and she's worried because Beau didn't come home after work and didn't call and isn't answering his phone. Do you know anything? Has he talked to you today?"

"Not today. I don't know why he would call *me*. Did she call the detective yet?"

"She said she called, but he—I think it was Detective Snaza —told her it was too soon to make a missing person's report. And so she called me, but I haven't heard from him either."

"I don't know what to tell you, Chip."

"Would you at least call Allison? I'll text you her contact info."

"Sure, but I don't know what I can do to help."

Julia shook her head as she ended the call. "I'm feeling like a missing person's bureau. That was Chip telling me about Beau not coming home, and he wants me to call Allison."

"Are you going to call her?"

"I guess, but as you'd say, it's really not my problem. And I don't know anything more than she does."

Allison picked up immediately when Julia called.

"Oh, thank you for calling me. Chip said he'd call you, and I realize you probably don't know either, but the police weren't any help, and I...I was frantic." She sniffled.

"I totally understand, Allison. You've already had one scare this week. Are you sure he's not in a meeting of some kind? Like, could he be meeting with his grad students?"

"Not on a Thursday. That's a Tuesday meeting."

"Staff meeting?"

"That was last week."

"Okay. What about his parents?"

"Gone. Dead."

"Brothers or sisters?"

"One sister. Lives in California and they're not close."

"Best friend? Hang out buddy?"

"I already called Ted, one of the other professors in his department. He hasn't seen him all day."

"What about his grad students? I remember one of them is named Laci Lia Ling, but I don't know the guy's name."

"It's Chase McGill, but I don't have direct contact info for the students. I've never had a reason to call either of them and if I did, I would call the office."

"Is Beau's laptop at the house? Maybe he has their numbers in his contact list."

"Let me check."

Julia heard sounds of shuffling paper, a chair scraping across the floor, and the thud of a soft bag of some kind.

"It's not here. He would normally have it with him at work, of course."

"Does he have a favorite bar where he goes sometimes?"

"If he does, I don't know what it is. He goes out to Ray's Boathouse sometimes, but that's usually for lunches with guests and that kind of thing. Since we had Benjamin, he comes home straight after work and plays with the kids till bedtime." Allison blew her nose.

"I don't know him as well as you do, but most likely, Beau will be home soon, and everything will be fine. With the scare you just had about your son, it is only natural to be anxious about most anything. Don't worry."

"Okay. You're probably right. Thanks, Julia. I feel better. I probably am overreacting. Goodbye."

"Good night, Allison."

Carly closed her book and set it on the table. "I wonder if he's with Sheldon and his thugs."

Julia frowned. "Why would he be with them?"

"They grabbed us earlier. Why not Beau? Maybe he's in on something with them."

"Hmm. As in, maybe he's a bad boy, too?" Julia said, her thoughts tumbling. "I don't want that to be the case."

Julia tried to watch the rerun of *NCIS* that she had queued up because she wasn't able to sleep. She had reassured Allison that Beau was fine. Now she had her doubts about that and about him as well. Plus, her brain kept going back to Lincoln and his calling Sheldon a traitor. There had to be more to the story that she hadn't heard yet. Had Beau left of his own accord? Was he with Laci Lia? Or not? What did he know that was so important to Sheldon? And who was Sheldon, anyway? Maybe knowing more about him was the key to solving the rest of the mystery.

CHAPTER
TWENTY-FIVE

Julia slept fitfully. Her unconscious mind brought up scenario after scenario of Beau in various kinds of trouble. At three a.m., she finally got out of bed and sat in a chair on the balcony with a blanket tucked around her. Being a sound sleeper in normal circumstances, she was surprised to discover how noisy the waterfront was during the last few hours before dawn. The first morning ferry runs, fishing boats heading out for the day, and even the cruise ships slinking into the harbor at the end of an Alaskan cruise created a cacophony of whistles and bells and low-pitched horns that accompanied the dawn.

At six, she went back inside and made some coffee using the in-room Keurig brewer and waited for Carly to wake up. She was ever so tempted to make some noise to hurry the process but decided to be nice, and curled up with her book instead until a more decent hour.

At six thirty she hopped into the shower after setting up a cup of coffee for her sister.

"Thanks for the coffee," said Carly when Julia emerged

clean-faced and scrubbed fifteen minutes later. "Why are you up so early?"

"Couldn't sleep. I just know Beau's in some kind of trouble. I had dream after dream of him, but I can't remember anything except snatches here and there."

"Chances are that he got home, and everything is okay. You can check with Allison and find out for yourself." Carly picked up her coffee and gathered her morning attire. "I'll be in the shower."

At seven thirty, Julia deemed it a reasonable hour to call Allison.

"He didn't come home, but he called and said he'd had to make a quick trip to San Diego," said Allison. "Something about retrieving some of his old notes that relate to the research he's doing at his lab here. I don't know why he wouldn't tell me about that ahead of time or at least call when it came up so I wouldn't worry. Anyway, I'm going to walk the kids to school. We haven't been letting them go by themselves since the kidnapping episode. He said he'd be home later today."

"I'm glad to hear it was something simple like that."

Julia heard Carly clearing her throat behind her as she ended the call. "Was that Allison?"

"Yeah. Beau called and said he had to make an unexpected trip to San Diego."

"Wouldn't he have told his wife about a trip like that?"

"You'd think so. I wonder if his office knew," said Julia. "Do you feel like going there to find out?"

"Can't you just call his secretary?"

"I could, but I want to see her facial reaction when I ask about him."

"Okay, then. Shall we grab a Starbucks breakfast and go over to the university as soon as we're both ready? You're still buying." Carly grabbed their bags and led the way out the door.

Friday morning traffic to the university was always crazy, but Julia knew how to get there without having to use the jammed freeway. She skimmed across town using Aurora Avenue to go north before crossing over to catch 40th Avenue East to the University District. She entered the campus from the south, as she had done so many times when she was a student. She was ecstatic to score a visitor pass with parking near the engineering building.

A mass of humanity was moving along the sidewalks from three directions into the building. Julia realized belatedly that she happened to hit campus a few minutes before the top of the hour, the typical class starting time. She and Carly waited outside the main entrance to allow the majority of the student traffic to settle down, then entered the building and found the stairs to Beau's second-floor departmental office.

Monica was at her station and looked up when Julia and Carly stepped through the door. She was sporting a navy tailored dress. She smiled and asked, "Can I help you two? Dr. Kennedy didn't tell me he was expecting anyone."

"I hope so," said Julia. "Is Dr. Kennedy in today?"

The woman's smile disappeared for a moment, then magically came back. "He's not in just yet, but I expect him any moment. He meets with two of his grad students at nine thirty every Friday morning."

Julia considered telling her about Allison's call but decided to play it cool for the moment. "When we met him here Tuesday, he introduced us to his students—Laci Lia Something is the one I'm thinking of. Is she here?"

"Laci Lia Ling," she said, smiling again. "Let me ring her

office." Ten rings later, she stood and said, "That's odd. I'll go see if she's in another room down the hall. Just one moment."

It was a long five minutes before she returned to her desk. "She's not here. Chase said he hasn't seen her. He just tried calling her, and she didn't answer. Neither did Beau when Chase tried his cell."

Julia and Carly looked at each other, eyebrows raised.

Monica narrowed her eyes. "Do you two know something about what's going on?"

Julia gave Monica an edited version of Beau's disappearance, grateful that Beau had already shared Benjamin's earlier disappearance with his secretary. Her sixth sense told her not to say anything about his supposedly going to San Diego. "I don't know if this is all connected, but I'm going to call Detective Monroe and update him on the circumstances. Can I use Dr. Kennedy's office to make the call?"

"Yes. Yes, of course. Please come in. I'll get you ladies some coffee."

JULIA AND CARLY sat with Detective Monroe in Beau's office. He had prickled when Julia called him but agreed to meet her in view of the inconsistencies that she had laid out. The office decor was starkly utilitarian except for the photographs of Allison and Benjamin and the twin girls, Sydney and Rylie, on the credenza. Everything was neatly organized on the top of his standard-issue college professor's wooden desk.

Julia had peeked in the desk drawers while waiting for Monroe to arrive. The files were in alphabetical order, the typed labels proudly announcing the contents of each folder. Except one in the very back of the second drawer. The handwritten label read *"Sealab"* in neat engineer's printing. One of Julia's colleagues at work had been a civil engineering major before entering medical school. She marveled at his ability to print such tiny yet legible letters. The folder was empty.

"Do you have any idea what might be going on with Dr. Kennedy?" Monroe asked, his notepad balanced on his knee. Julia had already given him an update of the calls with Chip and Allison and what she had learned so far at the office, which was zilch unless she counted the empty file folder.

Julia leaned back in Beau's leather chair, well-worn from his years as a professor. "I can't help but think Sheldon and his gang are behind Lincoln's attack, Benjamin's kidnapping, and Beau's disappearance somehow. I think Beau and Lincoln are at the center of this whole situation."

"Sheldon mentioned the nuclear conference and knew we had been there for Beau's lecture," said Carly. "Maybe that's the connection."

"Do you think Beau and this grad student, Laci Lia, are together?" asked Monroe.

"I think it's logical to assume that, yes," said Julia. "But are they willing participants in something? Did Sheldon round them up like he did Carly and me? Maybe they're hiding from Sheldon or someone."

"We could be looking at this from the wrong angle," said Carly. "What if Laci Lia is behind all this, and she's working with Sheldon? And maybe Beau has some information relevant to something involving *Sealab*."

Julia picked up the *Sealab* file folder from the desk and handed it to Monroe. "I found this empty file folder in the drawer. It's the only one that has a handwritten label, and it was out of alphabetical order. The fact that it's empty might be a clue, although it's possible it's been empty for a long time."

Monroe examined the dark green file. "It has a rounded bottom which suggests there was a thick file of papers in here at one time. My guess is that it was emptied very recently."

"Maybe Laci Lia emptied it instead of Beau," said Julia.

"Or his other grad student, Chase McGill," said Carly. "Why wouldn't both students be working on Beau's projects?"

Monroe sat back in his chair, elbows on the armrests, hands together with his fingers in a steeple shape. "It seems our next step has to be to track down Dr. Kennedy and Ms. Ling. I can have their phones pinged. I'll ask them directly about any connection to Sheldon Stanley."

"What about talking with Chip Englund?" asked Julia. "He's had contact from someone claiming to be involved with *Sealab* also. And he mentioned the cyber hack attempt at Jim Creek."

"Tell you what," said Monroe. "I'm giving you permission to chat with Mr. Englund. He may be more likely to reveal information to you than a cop, assuming he has something useful in his back pocket. Are you willing to do that?" He looked at Julia, then Carly. "And report back to me whatever he might say?"

Julia and Carly nodded at each other. "Yes, detective. We can do that." Julia added, "I certainly got the impression he knew something else, but wasn't ready to share what that is when we talked earlier."

Monroe checked his watch. "It's a few minutes after ten. What say we touch base in a couple of hours and share what we know?"

Monroe and Julia left their business cards with Monica as the threesome left the office and headed out on their respective assignments.

"Hɪ, Chip. This is Julia Fairchild. Do you have a minute?"

"What's on your mind?"

Julia shared the latest incident about Beau and Laci Lia

both being gone. "Of course, I don't have any proof, just a gut feeling, but it seems like *Sealab* is somehow at the bottom of this. What do you think?"

Chip coughed. After a short pause, he said, "I'm on my way to Bangor right now."

"You mean the submarine base on the peninsula?"

"Yes. Are you still in Seattle? I'm about twenty minutes from your hotel if you want to go with me. I'll explain more on the way."

"Carly, too?"

"Of course. I'll pick you up, and we'll drive over from there."

"We're on our way to the hotel from the university as I speak. I'm taking Aurora Avenue. ETA is about ten minutes. We'll meet you in the lobby."

"I don't remember this being on our Friday agenda," said Carly after Julia ended the call.

"The only definite item was the laser show tonight," said Julia. "What else would you rather be doing today?" She winked at her sister as they drove.

Carly rolled her eyes and said, "Something other than detective work."

"I hope Chip can give us some direction. He's the one other person with a possible connection to *Sealab*, even if it was indirect."

"Don't you think he's told us everything he knows already?"

"I never believe that," said Julia. "When I'm asking questions of my patients, I often have to be very creative to get the bottom-line answer of what's really going on. We humans have a tendency to want to hold back, even a little, instead of revealing everything we know." Julia maneuvered her car, nicknamed "White Stallion," onto southbound Aurora Avenue and merged into traffic. Everyone seemed to be going some-where in a hurry.

"Why is that?"

"Maybe we don't want to be judged, or we're afraid what we're thinking might be incorrect, or...I don't know. But it's human nature."

"Or someone might be keeping secrets."

TWENTY-SIX

The shortest route from Seattle to the Bangor Trident Submarine Base near Bangor, Washington was via the Washington State ferry system. With luck on their side, they caught the next ferry to Bainbridge Island with a few minutes to spare. Once they docked at Eagle Harbor, Chip merged into the traffic heading northward across the island on State Highway 305.

The drive from the ferry landing to Bangor was a little over thirty miles, with beautiful scenery along the entire route. Carly said, "I feel a bit of déjà vu. We drove much of this same road earlier in the week."

Chip glanced at Carly. "You did? Why were you over here?"

"We had cousins who lived here when we were growing up," said Carly. "We wanted to see what the island was like now. It has changed a lot in those twenty-five years."

Julia said, "More like eighty years, which was when the Japanese strawberry farmers and their families were forced from their homes and relocated to an internment camp in

Minidoka, Idaho. Only because they were Japanese and were presumed to be a possible threat after the bombing of Pearl Harbor. They were the first Japanese in the country to be moved by the federal government."

"I didn't know that," said Chip.

"We heard about it from Uncle Bill and Aunt Ethel. Our aunt grew up on the island and knew some of the people who left. She told us how the Filipino American community helped keep some of the strawberry farms running for three years until the owners could come back. Some came back but most didn't."

"That's a sad story when it touches so close to home," said Chip.

"I read about a beautiful Japanese American Exclusion Monument built not that long ago as a memorial. It's near the ferry terminal in Eagle Harbor."

"I'll check that out on another visit to Bangor. Thank you for adding that personal touch to the story."

Julia said, "Speaking of the ferry, I just thought of something. When we rode the ferry back that day to Seattle, we saw Sheldon and a couple of his friends. They disappeared into the crowd when we landed, so I didn't see where they went after that. Do you suppose they had gone to Bangor?"

Chip tilted his head. "I don't know how that could have helped them. They wouldn't be able to get through security and all that."

"Why are *you* going to the submarine base?" asked Julia. "I thought your job was more with the nuclear reactor sites."

"On a normal day, that would be true," he replied. "Today's not a normal day, however."

"Meaning what?"

"One of the senior leaders at Bangor got an email yesterday

with an ISP that suggests it came from the same place as the ones that tried to hack into Jim Creek."

"Do you mean *Sealab Four*?" asked Julia.

"Yes. *That* Sealab."

"Can you tell me what the email was about?"

"It's not so much what it was about, as where it came from."

"What was it about? Can you tell me?"

"It was a typical threatening type of message. We get them all the time." Chip smiled at Julia. "But this one came from an unusual source, and that's why Peter Manning, the senior commander there, asked me to come in person."

"I presume the submarine base has a ton of security. Will they let Carly and me in?"

"As long as you're with me, the answer is yes. I can vouch for you."

Julia's phone buzzed with detective Monroe's name. "Hi, Monroe. Julia here. We're with Chip Englund and headed to the Trident base at Bangor."

"Let me know what you find out. I just got word that Lincoln Wellsmith might also be missing. His sister Perdita called a while ago and said he left the house while she had gone to get groceries. He didn't leave a message and isn't answering his phone."

"Just like Beau and Laci Lia," said Julia. "What next?"

"I'm going over to the sister's house to do an evidence search. Let me know if you learn anything at Bangor. And call me around two o'clock either way."

"What did the detective have to say?" asked Carly when Julia ended the call. "What's 'just like Beau and Laci Lia?'"

"Lincoln has entered the missing persons portal. No message. And not answering his phone."

A gloomy silence settled in the car for the last fifteen minutes of the drive. The scenery along the remainder of the drive from Poulsbo to the submarine base was lush and green. The traffic was scanty. Julia's heart filled with dread as they neared the facility.

As Chip had predicted, Julia and Carly were allowed to enter the base as Chip's guests. Chip drove directly to the building where the commander's office was housed, and they were scrutinized again. Once they passed clearance, the threesome entered the secure office of the base commander, Peter Manning.

The office was small, with no external window. Julia wondered if that was because of the nature of the facility. The commander's desk was military-issue, with a large metal credenza to his left. The wall behind him was plastered with commendations and certificates. He had been in the Navy for at least twenty-five years, Julia guesstimated based on the dates. He was tall, six foot or so, and trim, with thinning, gray-tinged dark hair and a charming smile. One photo on the credenza showed him with his family. The wife's clothing and hair suggested it was taken ten to fifteen years earlier. The two boys appeared to be about six and eight.

"Thank you for seeing us," said Julia, after introductions were done by Chip. "Nice family." She pointed to the photo. "Your sons must be in college by now."

Commander Manning smiled broadly. "Yes, indeed. Brock, the older one, is in the Naval Academy. He wants to pursue a career in aerospace engineering."

"So why the Naval Academy instead of going into the Air Force?"

"They have an amazing program, surprisingly enough. He

wants to follow in my footsteps as far as being in the Navy goes. The younger boy, Troy, is leaning toward a future in law, but maybe I can redirect him before he goes too far down that road." Manning chuckled.

"Good luck with that, sir. My parents tried to keep me from going to medical school, but I found my way there anyway."

"So, how can I help you today?" He walked around his desk and sat on the corner, one leg on the floor and the other dangling, facing his small audience.

"Of course, you know about the activity at Jim Creek trying to get into our submarine communications center," said Chip.

"Yes. It was discussed at our weekly debriefing last week and again yesterday. How would that concern Dr. Fairchild and Miss Pedersen?" He glanced at the sisters.

Julia spoke for the two of them. "Last week, my sister and I found a near-dead gentleman at the arboretum near the university in Seattle. We had seen him the evening before with some men who showed up again at a nuclear conference, specifically at a lecture about *Sealab*, a couple of days later. On Tuesday, Carly and I were on the Bainbridge Island ferry when we thought we saw those same men again. And I got a photo of one of them. When the man we found at the arboretum, Lincoln Wellsmith, woke up, he recognized the man in that photo and said he was a traitor."

"So far, interesting, but nothing that involves us at Bangor," said Manning.

Chip added, "With that photo and other research, we determined that Sheldon Stanley is the man Julia has seen."

Julia continued, "And yesterday Sheldon and two other men kidnapped Carly and me from our hotel and threatened us. He was fishing for information about Lincoln and *Sealab*. And a friend of both Chip's and mine, Dr. Beau Kennedy, a nuclear engineering professor at the University of Washington who worked on the *Sealab* projects, disappeared last night. As did his grad student, Laci Lia Ling, who's from China. Beau's wife said he called her to say that he'd had to go to San Diego, but she said it was an unplanned trip and she's suspicious about it."

Manning said, "I've met Dr. Kennedy. Decent guy."

"Beau has gotten emails recently from an entity that says it's *Sealab Four*."

Chip nodded. "There does seem to be some kind of linkage between Dr. Kennedy, Mr. Wellsmith and Mr. Stanley that connect them all to *Sealab*. I don't know what it is, but there are too many references to *Sealab* to think they are all completely random."

Manning stood and walked back to his chair. He leaned back and exhaled loudly. "I'd like to see the photos you have of this Sheldon person, Dr. Fairchild. We can do a facial recognition search in our database. Maybe he'll show up. Our IT team is actively searching the dark web for other information on the so-called *Sealab Four*."

Julia pulled up the photo and handed her phone to the commander so he could forward it. When he handed it back, she scrolled to the photo of Lincoln that she'd taken at the arboretum just in case his face also popped up in the commander's database.

Manning stood and said, "Thank you. Ladies, I'm going to ask you to wait in the outer office while I keep Dr. Englund for a few more minutes. Have a pleasant day."

Julia and Carly sat in a pair of industrial waiting room chairs under the watchful eye of a young man dressed in his Navy summer whites. They were too far away to hear any of the conversation between the two men behind the closed door.

"I wish I were a mouse in that room," said Julia.

"That office was so sterile a mouse wouldn't survive. No food crumbs anywhere."

Julia chuckled and checked her watch. "Time to call Monroe. I wish I had more to report."

"I wish I had food. Can we ask Chip to stop for lunch on the way back?"

CHAPTER
TWENTY-SEVEN

Julia felt uncomfortable talking to the detective in the car in Chip's presence, so she texted him instead and said she'd call when she got back to the hotel.

During the drive back to Seattle, Chip stayed mum about whatever he and Commander Manning discussed. Julia was a bit miffed but reminded herself that she wasn't in the ranks of those privileged with knowing sensitive information. She and Carly were happy that he was willing to make a stop at The Loft at Latitude Forty Seven Seven in Poulsbo for lunch. Julia wondered if her offer to pony up was the deciding factor. Her stomach was growling its approval of a food refill.

"Do you think Commander Manning took our concerns seriously, Chip?" Julia asked.

"Yes and no. He recognizes that there's some traffic on the web, but so far, nothing has risen to the level of credible impending danger. The submarine base remains on high alert as always, until there's a discernible change in chatter."

"Is he worried about Beau Kennedy?"

"He didn't say so in so many words. He's more concerned

about the grad student, Laci Lia. Her uncle is reportedly in the Chinese military, which is notoriously corrupt. They've been known to take big monetary bribes and look the other way. The Chinese government has been making some progress in its conversations with the United States government to reach some kind of peace deal. They're worried about anything that might interfere with the talks."

"Are you saying Laci Lia might be a problem?" asked Julia.

Chip shook his head. "Not her. Her uncle."

"Could she be in danger?" asked Carly.

"Does she know something she shouldn't?" asked Julia.

"We don't know that yet," said Chip. "But someone might think she does, which is equally dangerous for her. We need to find her and Dr. Kennedy. The sooner, the better."

"Who's 'we'?" asked Julia.

"You didn't hear me say this, but the CIA is actively involved in the search."

"The CIA? Why?"

"All I can tell you is that there's been a breach, and we believe one of their agents has gone rogue."

"I feel like I'm in an episode of *FBI International*," said Carly.

Julia saw Chip glance at her sister in the back seat and grimace as Julia said, "I marvel at how they always manage to solve those crimes in that one-hour time slot."

"Scriptwriters have no sense of reality," said Carly. "They live in an imaginary world all the time."

Chip managed a grim smile. "We're hoping to find them quickly, of course, but it will probably take more than an hour. We're not allowed to use scriptwriters."

"Are we allowed to know who the agent is?" asked Julia.

Chip turned toward Julia and narrowed his eyes. "I'll pretend I didn't hear that. Here's that lunch spot."

. . .

Julia's salmon cakes and Carly's and Chip's burgers were excellent, as was the view of the water traffic. They witnessed several seaplanes land and take off again while they ate.

"I just thought of something," said Julia once they were back on the road. "Those seaplanes would be another way that someone could get in and out of an area quickly without using a car or other public transportation."

"They could also go by boat," said Carly. "Although they couldn't go as far or as fast as a small plane."

"Who do you have in mind for this sudden getaway?" asked Chip.

"What if that's how someone spirited Beau and Laci Lia away? Maybe Sheldon got to them as he did to us?"

"I don't see how that would help him, although there are several seaplane companies around Seattle with stops on Lake Washington and Lake Union and elsewhere."

"They could just be hiding somewhere, like in a warehouse," said Carly. "We don't have any proof that they've left Seattle."

"The police are checking video footage on and near the university campus," said Chip. "I haven't heard anything of the results, though."

"What about Lincoln? He was staying with his sister, so maybe there are some cameras in her neighborhood," said Julia.

Chip swiveled his head toward Julia. "Trust me. They're on it."

Julia's shoulders slumped. "I feel so helpless. I wish I could help more."

"You've been more observant than most people would be,"

said Chip. "There are a lot of eyes looking for Beau and Laci Lia. We'll find them."

Back at the Edgewater, Julia and Carly checked their respective emails and messages.

Julia shrieked. "There's a text message here from Beau. He must have gotten access to his phone."

"What does he say?"

"He says there's a file in his desk drawer at work. It's labeled 'Bens.' He wants us to find it and give it to the detective." Julia checked the time. "It's still early enough in the day that Monica should be there, even on a Friday. I'll call her and let her know we'll be there in about twenty minutes."

"Could he have sent it from his watch? I know you can receive texts on your Fitbit, but can you send them?"

"I've never tried, but I heard you can do it from an Apple watch. A couple of the guys at the clinic are always bragging about them. I need to call Monroe."

Julia briefed Monroe on the visit to the submarine base and told him about the message from Beau. "We're going to go to his office and see if we can find this file he mentioned."

"Call me if you find anything," he replied.

"Did you hear from Beau?" asked Monica as soon as they entered the nuclear engineering department office. "Is he okay? What about Laci Lia?"

Julia shook her head. "We got a text message, but we didn't actually get to talk with him. It said to look in his drawer for a folder labeled 'Ben.'"

"Ben? His son?"

"I guess so. Can we take a look for it?"

"He has several file cabinets full of stuff, but there's also a file drawer in his desk."

"I'll check his desk files first," said Julia. "It seems more logical that he would keep information about his son closer at hand. Carly, will you tackle that tall file cabinet in the corner?"

Monica said, "I'll check the smaller cabinet in his conference room."

A few minutes later, Julia said, "I've found a file."

Carly said, "So did I. Now what?"

"Now we look through them and see if there's something useful. One of them might really be about his son, and the other could be something else."

Monica finished her search without finding a folder, so she watched over Julia's shoulder while Julia quickly thumbed through the papers jammed into the manila folder. "This one seems to be all about his son. I'm not seeing anything unusual. Carly, are you having better luck?"

"Yep. It looks like Beau practiced a little subterfuge here. This folder is full of information that must have come from his work at Scripps." She showed Julia the label. "It's BENS, not Ben."

Julia smiled as she read the tiny handwritten subtitle: "Beau: Engineering, Nuclear: Sealabs. Of course! BENS is the acronym for these records, which I'm guessing are from his work at Scripps. I wonder if he moved this material here after getting the emails from *Sealab Four*."

"He might not have even trusted his grad students if they knew that he had worked on this project in the past," said Carly.

"Especially Laci Lia, considering she's Chinese and has an uncle working in the Chinese military," said Julia. "Now we have to let Detective Monroe know, and probably Chip, too.

There must be something in here that someone thinks is worth stealing. But what and why?"

"What about the other grad student? The guy named Chase."

Julia paused and thought for a moment. "As far as we know, he doesn't have a direct connection to the Chinese. But Laci Lia does, which makes her more suspicious. At least to me."

"And he isn't missing. Commander Manning needs to know, too, don't you think?" asked Carly.

"Certainly. He'll probably want the CIA involved."

Monica asked, "How are you going to keep this information safe until you give it to Dr. Englund or somebody?"

"I'm dialing Monroe right now," said Julia. "I don't want to be responsible for it, and it's probably not safe here, either."

"Yes, Detective," said Julia when he answered. "We found the material that might have been in that empty *Sealab* folder. I think you'll want to come get it and keep it safe. Whoever has Beau and Laci Lia might come back and get it without asking anyone's permission."

Julia looked at Monica and nodded. "Carly and I will be here with the department secretary until you arrive."

Monica set about tidying the office for the weekend. "I'll stay here with you until the detective arrives. I can't leave the office unattended, as I'm sure you understand." She glanced at the clock on the wall. "It's already four thirty, so I hope he can be here by five. I have plans for the evening." Her cheeks turned a lovely shade of pink.

Julia split the folder contents into two piles and said to Carly, "We might as well look through this stuff while we're waiting. Maybe we'll find something that will crack the case."

"I'm holding you to the laser light show tonight, Julia, so we'd better solve it quickly."

CHAPTER
TWENTY-EIGHT

The office clock was the type that had an audible "tick" every second. "How do you tolerate that ticking?" Julia asked Monica after five minutes of sixty ticks each and every minute.

"The clock? I don't even hear it anymore unless I let it enter my consciousness. Or when it seems like time is dragging by and I want to leave the office." She winked.

"This might be something, Julia," said Carly, looking up from a paper she had been perusing. "Wasn't an oxygen supply the biggest hurdle for the early *Sealab* experiments?"

"Yes, I believe it was."

"This was written by Beau. It looks like a thesis or something. Here."

Julia thumbed through the document of about thirty pages. It had been typed in the standard double-space format of the day. "A lot of this is research regurgitation, but the bottom line is that a functional *Sealab* needs to have its own electrolysis system to create oxygen from seawater, as is done on submarines."

The room was quiet except for the ticking of the clock for the next several minutes while the sisters scanned article after article.

"It would sure help to know what we're looking for," said Carly. "Too bad Beau didn't send a longer message."

"I've got something," said Julia. "It's a letter from Scripps to Beau. The date on it is 2010, so about twelve years ago. And it's signed by Lincoln Wellsmith!" Julia looked at Carly. "Didn't Beau say he didn't know Lincoln?"

"Lincoln said he knew Beau and that sometimes they had drinks together with Sheldon."

"So another fib."

"Plus, we showed him his picture from when we found him at the arboretum," said Carly.

"True, but Lincoln looked beat up, and that was more a side shot of his head. I suppose a letter from him doesn't prove that he knew what he looked like," said Julia, sighing. "Did we ever tell Beau that Lincoln woke up and remembered more details about that night?"

"Maybe. I'm not sure. So tell me already what the letter is about."

"It looks like Beau had written to Scripps about some of his research results. He apparently wanted some detail about a project that he could use in his doctoral thesis. But there isn't anything specific in this letter."

"Hm. Maybe there was an attachment at some time with those results."

"Maybe," said Julia. "Let's keep checking."

Another fifteen minutes passed by, accompanied by the annoying ticking clock. Julia jumped when she heard Detective Monroe knock on the door just before he entered.

"Did you find anything helpful?" he asked when he noticed the open file folder.

"Not really," said Julia. "We found a letter from Lincoln to Beau when Lincoln was working at Scripps, but there wasn't anything useful in the letter itself." Julia resumed shuffling through the final few papers in her half of the file.

"Except it kinda proves that they weren't unknown to each other," said Carly.

"Bingo," said Julia. "I found something. Here's a hand-written note. It says, 'Be careful of what you say around Chip.'"

"Who sent it?" asked Monroe.

"No signature and no date," said Julia. "It's torn off from a bigger piece of paper, like a letter-size notepad."

"Is it the same writing as on the letter from Lincoln?" asked Carly.

"Doesn't look like it to me," said Julia.

Monica said, "Maybe I can tell who wrote it, if you don't mind my looking at it."

Julia handed the note to Monica, who pursed her lips as she studied the message.

"I'm not sure, but it looks familiar," said Monica. "When Beau first started here, he had just finished his doctorate and got letters occasionally from somebody he'd worked with at Scripps. He goes there now about once a month for a couple of days because of his dual appointment."

"It might not matter who wrote it," said Monroe, "especially if it was written years ago, as is certainly possible. It does inform us that Chip might not be fully trustworthy, however. I'll take what's here and go through it more carefully at the station."

Monica checked the time. "I can't stay any later, and I can't leave you here alone."

"Is Chase in his office?" asked Julia.

"I'm sorry, but he's already gone for the day. I'm the last one here."

Julia and Carly assembled the pile of letters and documents into a single stack and put them back into the file labeled BENS.

"We can look at the rest of this file at the office. I'll let my staff tackle it, and maybe we'll be able to track the source of that message," said Monroe. "Can you meet me at the station?"

Julia and Carly looked at each other and at the clock. Julia said, "As long as we can get to the laser show at the Seattle Center sometime tonight."

"This is Jesse Cochran," said Monroe when Julia and Carly arrived at the station. "He's a whiz at all things technical and triangular, as in the triangulation of cell towers. I told him about your message from Beau, and he'll take a stab at locating the source."

Julia handed over her phone after unlocking it and finding the message for Jesse.

Monroe disappeared into his office, leaving Julia and Carly in the outer lobby while Jesse fiddled with his bank of computers.

"It would help to know how long that note about Chip has been in Beau's possession," said Julia. "It could be recent, which could signify some recent revelation, or from years back, but that doesn't make as much sense. Why would Beau still consider Chip a good friend if he's had that note a long time?"

"I bet it's more recent," said Carly, "and that's why Beau moved the *Sealab* material to a different file."

"I tend to agree with you. But why or how would Chip have access to Beau's private files? So, the next obvious challenge is to figure out who wrote it. And when? And why is it in Beau's file?"

"What if someone at the nuclear energy conference a few

days ago passed it to Beau? That would explain why it was on that kind of paper."

"Makes as much sense as anything, but who would that be?" Julia slumped in her chair, arms and legs crossed, her right foot tapping silently in the air.

"As I recall, when Beau gave his lecture, the room was dark for the powerpoint presentation, and when the lights came back on, some people had already left the room. Like Sheldon and his friends."

"And several of the attendees went up to Beau afterward and talked with him," said Julia. "Maybe one of them slipped him the note."

"But they would have to have known that Beau knew Chip."

"I think Sheldon and Lincoln both fit in that category, just from the way Beau talked," said Julia, "even though he didn't admit to knowing either of them at first."

"Isn't the nuclear engineering world a finite universe? Chip made a comment at one point about seeing some of the same people at another conference recently."

"True. Beau could have gotten that note from someone at a different meeting or at any other time."

A few minutes later, Jesse, the IT specialist, emerged from his corner with a frown on his face. Julia and Carly jumped up to meet him at the counter.

"Miss Fairchild, I triple-checked the results because I couldn't believe what I was seeing. This email originated from a source called *Sealab Four*. Does that make any sense to you?"

CHAPTER

TWENTY-NINE

"Yes. Sort of. I've heard of it. Thank you." Julia stared at her phone for a moment in disbelief before tucking it in her pocket. "Do you suppose we could speak with Detective Monroe again for a moment?"

Monroe stepped out of his office and motioned to the sisters to join him. "I overheard Jesse say the message purportedly came from *Sealab*. Do you have any idea what that means?"

Julia sighed and shook her head. "Not exactly. I'm beginning to believe it's an elaborate scam of some kind."

"It's like some gigantic invisible web that has surrounded Beau and Chip, and maybe Lincoln and Sheldon," said Carly.

"But it's gotta mean something," said Julia. "Each of those men has a link to *Sealab*, regardless of how remote it might be. What is that missing link?"

"Remember when Chip told us about the attempt to hack into the Jim Creek Communication system? That's like the center of the universe in the underwater submarine world. What if that's the link to everything?"

155

"Yeah, but how would we find out?" asked Carly.

"I'm retired from the Navy," said Monroe. "I'll call and see if I can get permission to talk with Commander Manning. This could be one more piece of the puzzle. Someone is trying to get a message out, whoever it is. I'll let you ladies wait in the lobby with the desk sergeant while I make a couple of calls."

JULIA AND CARLY cooled their heels once again, with Carly keeping her eye on the clock behind the desk sergeant's head. As it moved ever so slowly, she said, "At least this clock doesn't tick every second like Monica's clock."

"You wouldn't mind terribly if we had to wait till tomorrow to see the laser show, would you, sis?" Julia reached over and patted Carly's knee. "I know we both really want to see it, but we could stay over another night if we have to. Right?"

Carly rolled her eyes. "As if I really have a choice."

Julia sat up straighter. "There's Monroe. He has a little smile on his face."

The detective waved and invited them into his office for round two. "Interesting developments we have going on," he said as he sat down in his well-worn leather office chair. "Chip has been sending messages through a series of networks to make it look like they're coming from *Sealab*."

"Chip? Are you sure?" Julia furrowed her brows. "He doesn't seem the type."

"Commander Manning told me the CIA has been watching him for a while. In fact, that's the reason he asked him to come to the submarine base yesterday. Manning had planned to give him some information, false information, that is, about an intervention coming up at Bangor in an attempt to see if Chip leaked any of that to suspected colleagues of his in the Chinese military."

"Did we screw it up by being with Chip?" asked Julia. "He asked us to join him when we called him earlier about Beau and Laci Lia being missing."

"No. Not at all. In fact, the information you shared with the commander was helpful in filling a couple of gaps." Monroe leaned forward on his desk. "Did Chip tell you anything about what Manning said to him?"

Julia and Carly looked at each other, then Julia said, "He said something about a CIA agent going rogue and how it was imperative that Dr. Kennedy and Laci Lia be found soon."

"Okay. So, he took the bait."

Julia scowled. "Is that what he was supposed to share? Was that false information?"

Monroe smiled. "I'm not going to tell you, for obvious reasons. I trust you will call me if you hear from Chip?"

"Yes, sir," said Julia. "Of course we will. Are we free to go?"

"Yes. I'm sorry I kept you. You could still take in the late laser show at the Seattle Center if you hurry."

"WHAT DO you think about having a quick bite at one of the fast food stands now and getting something more substantial after the show?" Julia negotiated the traffic heading from downtown Seattle to the Seattle Center, a short 1.6-mile drive of about ten minutes, while Carly looked up ticket information on her cell.

"The Billie Eilish show starts at nine o'clock and runs about an hour," said Carly. "We can make it to that showing and still have time to eat a snack if we're there in the next fifteen minutes. I'll get tickets."

"Okay. We'll be on time. Traffic's moving nicely on a busy Friday night. For a change."

Julia and Carly wolfed down chili dogs and Pepsis at the

first food stand they saw. They were standing at the entrance to the Laser Dome, ready to enter, when Julia's cell signaled a text message's arrival. "It's from Monroe. He says Laci Lia has been located. She had taken the day off to help a friend shop for a wedding dress."

"Sounds reasonable enough," said Carly. "What about Beau?"

"Laci Lia didn't know anything about why he wasn't in the office."

"So, it was just a coincidence that they were both gone, unannounced?"

"Apparently, but it still sounds fishy to me." Julia turned the phone to mute. "Let's go watch the show. I can't imagine anything disastrous happening in the next hour."

THE STARS SHONE brilliantly against the midnight blue sky, despite the city lights that tried to penetrate the blackness, when Julia and Carly emerged from the Laser Dome. The din of the traffic noise was almost deafening after the hour of amazing lights with spirals and bolts and spinning stars set to the engaging music of Billie Eilish.

"That was absolutely incredible!" said Carly. "I don't even know where to begin to try to describe those lights and beams and all the movements within the show. I've never seen anything like that." Her voice bubbled with excitement, and she used her hands to demonstrate the movement of the light beams.

"Truly a heart-lifting experience," said Julia as they walked toward the car. She fiddled with her phone for a moment while waiting for the signal to change at the crosswalk. "Here's another message from Monroe. He wants me to call even if it's late. It's about Lincoln."

"What now, for Pete's sake?"

Julia smiled kindly at her sister while she made the call. "Hi, Detective. What's going on with Lincoln? Did you find him?"

"He found us, actually. He said he'd been following up on some email traffic that he stumbled on at Scripps. He finally remembered why he had decided to join Sheldon at the nuclear energy conference. Dr. Kennedy's name showed up repeatedly in the emails that were being sent to a technology lab in Qingdao, China."

"What else?"

"Lincoln, who also happens to have a Ph.D. in nuclear engineering, believes the Chinese government is enhancing its nuclear submarine fleet. That lab, which is right on the coast directly across from South Korea, is a counterpart to Scripps Institution of Oceanography and is the main center for experimentation involving submarines."

"Wow. But Beau worked at Scripps at least ten years ago. Why would those emails be important now?"

"You've heard Dr. Kennedy's student Laci Lia Ling has an uncle in the Chinese government. Correct?"

"Yes. Are you thinking she and Beau are involved in something fishy?"

"That's a concern. Commander Manning shared with me that the Chinese military is notoriously corrupt and that Miss Ling's uncle is in charge of their submarine division."

"Oh. That's huge. Do you have any idea whether Beau or Laci Lia is involved in anything illegal?"

"We don't know yet. Mr.—I mean Dr. —Englund hasn't been forthcoming about some of the details that we've traced to his *Sealab* emails."

"Okay." Julia took a big breath. "Is there something you

want me—or Carly and me—to do? I can't imagine how we could help at this point."

"I didn't tell you yet that Dr. Kennedy called his wife a little while ago. He'd made a quick trip to San Diego. Told her he needed something from his files at his old research lab and didn't want to worry her. He said he'd left his cell in his car accidentally. Of course, we're checking airlines to verify his story."

"She told us something like that when I called her this morning," said Julia. "I must have forgotten to tell you. But didn't you ping his phone?"

"We tried. I suspect he had turned off the GPS locator. A lot of people do that to save battery life. Anyway, he's due back this evening within the hour."

"What is it you need us to do?" asked Julia.

"Set up a meeting with him tomorrow around lunchtime. We want to get him away from his house and office for a couple of hours. Allison—Mrs. Kennedy—has agreed to take her son to the zoo so we can search his home office."

"Wow. That must have taken some doing. Why would she agree to that?"

"I explained that we're looking for evidence that he's being blackmailed. She bought that story."

"I'm not buying it," said Julia.

"I can't tell you everything yet, Dr. Fairchild. Will you make a lunch date with Dr. Kennedy? Please?"

"Sure. I'll tell him I owe him a lunch. I'll let you know as soon as I have it set up."

Julia shared the details of the call with Carly. "It's way too late to call him now, think." She checked her watch. "It's almost eleven."

"You could text him. He can get back to you in the morning."

"Good idea." Julia sent the text message inviting Beau to meet her and Carly at the Capital Grille downtown at eleven thirty the next day. "I added that I owe him lunch and that it's our last day here."

"We can finish that bottle of wine while we wait to see if he texts back," said Carly. "I bet he responds tonight."

Julia's cell pinged a few minutes later with Beau's confirmation that he would be there.

"Here's to a few more hours of detective work before we head back home," said Julia as she raised her glass to Carly.

THIRTY

The weather had been beautiful the whole week, which was definitely an anomaly in Seattle, even with May being one of the drier months. Saturday dawned clear with a blue sky and a rare cloud.

"I really don't feel like packing to go home, but we have to check out before we meet Beau unless we decide to stay another night," said Julia.

"Maybe *you* aren't ready to go home," said Carly, "but I have plans for tomorrow with Rob, so I really can't stay any longer."

"I know. I go through this every time I have to end a vacation." Julia sighed. "At least I don't have to worry about how much my suitcase weighs this time. Not that we bought anything while we were here, anyway."

Carly groaned. "How is it that clothes get bigger and don't want to fit in the same suitcase going home? I remember this problem when we were packing to come home from Virgin Gorda."

Julia chuckled. "That's where tote bags come in handy. I

brought a couple of extra ones to use for the overflow." She tossed one to her sister. "You can use this one with the Seattle Seahawks logo on it. Rob will like it."

Carly held it up and smiled. "Yes, he will. Thanks."

The sisters cleared out the drawers and collected the miscellany that had scattered itself around the room during the week's stay.

"I think I've got my stuff pretty much ready to go," said Julia. "Are you ready to find some breakfast?"

"Give me five more minutes, and I'll be done."

Julia's phone buzzed in her back pocket, startling her. "It's Lincoln. I wonder what he wants."

"Maybe he remembered something else."

"Hi, Lincoln. Julia here. What's up?"

"Hello, Dr. Fairchild. I remember why I called Sheldon a traitor."

"Why was that?"

"He is working with the Chinese."

"Are you sure? Have you called Detective Monroe and told him?"

"I tried, but my call went straight to voice mail, and the dispatch officer said he was unavailable right now. That's why I'm calling you."

"Okay. I can relay the message. What shall I tell him?"

"I can't tell you over the phone. Can I meet you somewhere?"

"Sure. There's a coffee shop called Retro Coffee on 5th Avenue. Are you nearby?"

"I can be there in fifteen minutes. See you then."

"We'll check out of the hotel and be there as soon as we can." Julia stared at her phone for a moment as she relayed the plan to her sister. "The plot thickens."

• • •

JULIA AND CARLY found a table away from the handful of other patrons in the shop. Julia ordered a London Fog: Earl Gray tea mixed with coconut milk. She had grown very fond of the hot drink after being introduced to it by her friend Paula. Carly chose peppermint tea, unadorned.

"Are you going to ask Lincoln where he was yesterday when he left his sister's house?" asked Carly.

"Of course I am. I want to know where all the players were yesterday so we can narrow down the suspect list."

"Suspects for what? No one's been murdered. What's left to solve?"

"The messages from *Sealab Four* have to be important somehow," said Julia. "I wonder if they're a diversionary tactic of some kind."

"Or a prank," said Carly.

"And we don't know why Lincoln was assaulted. I'm fairly certain Sheldon had a hand in it, but why? What is Sheldon afraid of? What is he hiding?"

Carly said, "There's Lincoln now." She stood and waved at him where he stood in the doorway.

Lincoln scanned the faces in the coffee shop before approaching the table and sitting down. The waitress had been watching and quickly came over and took his order for green tea.

"Thank you for agreeing to meet me," said Lincoln. "I have been staying clear of Sheldon. That's why I left my sister's home. He had me tailed a couple of nights ago and showed up at the house the next day."

"What does he want from you?" asked Julia. "Are you mixed up in this *Sealab* story as well?"

Lincoln smiled thinly. "I was one of the Project Managers at Scripps at a time when we were finishing up the last of the research projects left over from the *Sealab* heyday. Dr. Kennedy was one of the last graduate students who got to do hands-on work with the old team. He was given permission to continue working on one of the biggest challenges after he finished his studies."

"What was that?" asked Julia.

"You may recall that hypothermia was a huge problem in the earlier *Sealab* projects. We had to find something other than helium to warm the interior if we were going to be able to build larger facilities underwater. Once that issue was solved, it would be feasible to go ahead with larger, improved *Sealabs*."

"Why is that important?" asked Carly. "Why aren't submarines enough for underwater living?"

Lincoln chuckled. "It's like trying to build cities on the moon or even Mars. Humans, by nature, want to conquer other worlds. Even some of the Greek and Roman Gods had dominion over the ocean—Neptune being the prime example as the god over the seas."

"But that's mythology," countered Julia. "Even the lost city of Atlantis is a myth."

"Not so fast, Dr. Julia," said Lincoln. "There are plenty of people who would argue with you that we simply haven't found it yet. The oceans have swallowed up plenty of land over the millennia. Why couldn't there be a lost city underwater?"

Carly scoffed. "The people would certainly be dead. So, what's the point of trying to reinvent this underwater world?"

Lincoln nodded. "I understand your skepticism, but there is a vast world under the surface that is ripe for exploration. What if we were able to build a gigantic, *Sealab*-like city underwater that could be a base for submarines? And those submarines could go anywhere. For example, maybe there's a passage under the ice north of Canada for travel to Europe instead of having to cut through the ice as we do now. Or have to go around South America."

"That's actually a little scary, in my opinion," said Julia. "It's creepy to think that these *Sealabs* could be miles underwater, and we might not know they were there. Or would we?"

"I'm sure someone somewhere is working on devices that would be able to do that kind of detection, but it's not available yet today."

"I don't want to think about it," said Julia. "So, Lincoln, what is it that you couldn't tell us over the phone?"

"I think you heard Beau—Dr. Kennedy—say that he thought he was nearing a breakthrough on his research in his lab here. It could potentially solve the hypothermia problem in an underwater environment."

"Wow. That's big," said Julia.

"Yes. And there's plenty of high-level interest in his work."

"So, it's not secret?" asked Carly.

"His methods are secret, but because of the way funding goes for research, and because he has reported on some of his earlier findings, other research scientists both in the United States and elsewhere have keen interest in his studies. Governments, too."

"Is there money involved?" Julia signaled for a second round of tea for all.

"Yes and no. Beau wouldn't own the rights to anything he discovers. He's an employee of the university, and they would hold any patents. He also has a dual appointment at the Scripps Institution of Oceanography, which you know is located in San Diego. Scripps would share in this patent and any financial rewards if there were any down the road."

"So, what's the problem?" asked Julia.

"We have reason to believe that Sheldon may be working with the Chinese government. He has been trying to persuade Beau to leave his university positions and join a private consortium. If he were to do that, he could make a fortune in the open market, assuming he solves the final piece of the problem."

"Do you think that's why Beau went to San Diego? To get information for Sheldon?"

"I hope not. He doesn't own the rights to his research, if he even went there. But he could conceivably walk away from what he's done so far and start over."

"Except he wouldn't be starting from the beginning," said Julia. "He would be able to streamline whatever he already knows and build on that. It's not like he's going to leave his brain behind."

"Yes, but right now, he's stressed with the kidnapping, even though his son has been returned, and his wife has learned about his affair with his graduate student."

"I was right," said Carly. "I knew he was up to something."

"I happen to know that Laci Lia, the student, worked with him at Scripps. He encouraged her to apply to his department. Working in such close proximity for some five years now comes with occupational hazards."

"Why are you telling us this?" Julia fiddled with her tea.

"I want you to understand that I believe Beau is loyal to his country and would not sell out to the highest bidder, but money is very tempting. I think the emails from *Sealab Four* are real and are meant to alarm Beau. You must persuade Detective Monroe to pursue the truth behind all of this."

"How? We don't have access to privileged information, and we're not detectives," said Julia.

"Yes, but you are very smart, and I trust you will figure this out."

Lincoln rose and gave a half-bow. "My sister will know where I am if you need me. Please help Beau."

Julia and Carly watched as Lincoln left the coffee shop.

"What now? I was ready to throw Beau under the bus," said Carly.

"Same here." Julia checked the time and grabbed her tote as she rose. "It's time to meet Beau at the Capital Grille. Maybe we'll learn something useful."

CHAPTER

THIRTY-ONE

Beau was waiting in a booth near the back of the restaurant. He waved when he spotted Julia and Carly and rose like a gentleman when they were within ten feet. Julia thought he looked a bit bedraggled, with circles under his eyes. He wore the engineering professor's uniform consisting of a tweed sports coat with khakis and a button-down shirt, minus a tie.

He greeted them with brief hugs and a lukewarm smile. "I didn't think I would be seeing you again. I thought you were leaving town yesterday."

"That was the original plan, but we had some glitches during the week, so we stayed over an extra day," said Julia.

"We hadn't seen the laser show at the Seattle Center yet, and Julia promised me that we could go. So, I guess it's kinda my fault." Carly flashed that radiant grin.

Beau sighed. "It's been a tough week for me, and maybe for you as well." He picked up a carafe of wine and poured it into the three glasses on the table. "I hope you like pinot grigio. The house wine here is usually good, especially the whites."

Julia smiled. "It makes it feel like a mini-celebration. Cheers to running into old friends!" She raised her glass.

Carly added, "And making new ones."

"By the way," said Beau, "I must thank you for getting the BENS file to the detective." He leaned forward and looked Julia in the eyes. "You did get it to him, didn't you?"

Julia nodded. "Of course. He took it down to his office instead of taking time to look through it at the university. I would think he would call you if he found something important." She sipped her wine before asking, "How has Benjamin been? Is he able to sleep and all? Has he been affected by the kidnapping at all?"

Beau shrugged. "He doesn't seem to have missed a beat. I think it bothered Allison and me more than our tough little guy."

"Do you know who was responsible yet?" asked Julia. "The money had to have been transferred somewhere. Is it traceable?"

"I don't know if you understand how the dark web works, but this kind of money transfer goes through a number of different sites before it gets to the final recipient. It's difficult to trace. My father-in-law says his company has already started working on it, but it could take months, and we may still never find out where it went."

"That's just wrong," said Carly.

"Yes, it is," said Beau. "Advances in technology come with huge price tags, including the bad guy's ability to hide behind many layers of screens and become virtually invisible."

"Enough of the dark web," said Julia. "This menu is making it hard to choose a meal. Beau, do you have any recommendations?"

"The seafood and steak options are all delicious. I think I've tried them all."

Julia opted for the clam chowder and a fresh salad, while Carly decided to try lobster bisque and the pan-fried calamari with hot cherry peppers. Beau ordered a man-sized ribeye steak sandwich with sautéed onions and cheddar.

"I hope you're going to tell me why you really wanted to meet me today, Julia," said Beau. "You were never good at fibbing, and I don't believe your story that you owed me a lunch." He refilled his glass and took a big swallow.

Julia felt her face turn pink as she tried to hide behind her own glass by taking a sip of her wine. "Yeah, I know I never had a good poker face. I admit I'm having a hard time understanding how Sheldon and Lincoln are mixed up in this whole *Sealab* affair. And Chip, too. You might remember that I like everything to make sense in the end, and I don't have that satisfaction yet."

Beau leaned back in his chair and looked up as if divining an answer from the ceiling. "Frankly, I think somebody—and I don't know who—is using the web just to make us think everything is coming from an imaginary *Sealab Four*."

"Do you think it's related to the research you said you're doing that might lead to a breakthrough in underwater survival?" Julia finished her wine and let Beau refill her glass.

"I don't know how or why it would. Our own government isn't interested enough to give us the money to finish what we started. So, what does that tell you?" Beau sat up straight again just as the waiter approached the table with a tray of food.

The aroma was a delectable blend of perfectly grilled steak and the seafood soups. Warm bread in a basket completed the olfactory buffet.

"Let's eat while it's warm," said Beau. He ordered a second carafe of wine and dug in.

After what Julia felt was a reasonable time to allow the

eating pace to slow, she asked Beau, "How long have you known Laci Lia?"

Beau coughed and wiped his lips with his napkin. "Laci Lia? About four years now. Ever since she applied for one of our graduate student positions."

"You didn't know her before?"

Beau shook his head and pursed his lips. "No. She was the top applicant for the open position that year, and we awarded it to her almost as soon as we met her for an in-person interview. She was that good." He sat back and smiled. "And she's proven to be as astute as I'd hoped."

Julia furrowed her brow. "Was there anyone besides you on the interview team?"

"Of course. Several department chairs and a couple of professors in the respective departments are responsible for doing the interviews and reviewing the applications. The chair of the specific department with the opening has the final say, although he would typically follow the recommendation of the team. Why do you ask?"

Julia and Carly looked at each other. Julia said, "I was just curious. Especially since she's a woman in a field that I suspect is almost exclusively male."

"But wasn't that true of you when you applied for medical school? I know the balance has shifted drastically over the past twenty years or more, but when you were a child, did you ever see a woman physician? What even made you think you could be one yourself?"

Julia smiled smugly. "My childhood ear doctor told me I should go to medical school when I told him I wanted to be a doctor like him. I was seven at the time." She shrugged. "So I did."

Beau nodded. "That's exactly the point I was trying to

make. Somebody saw potential in you, as someone else saw that Laci Lia could be a nuclear engineer." He finished his wine and poured a third glass, or was it his fourth? He checked the time, making a show of looking at his Rolex watch.

"Are you in a hurry? We won't keep you if you need to be someplace else," said Julia. She had figured if she kept Beau occupied until at least one o'clock, Detective Monroe and his team would have had enough time to do their house and office search. It would take Beau at least fifteen minutes to get to his office and twenty to thirty minutes to get to his home, depending on Saturday traffic. That meant she needed to keep him talking for another fifteen minutes. She refilled her glass halfway, and Carly's, too, winking at her sister as she did so.

"I don't think I've ever asked how you met your beautiful wife, Allison. It seems that she showed up out of the blue while we were at the university."

Beau's chest seemed to swell a little bigger with pride. "We met at an investment party that her father's business had thrown. One of my fraternity brothers dragged me there because he was worried that I wouldn't manage my money well and because there was free food and alcohol." He chuckled. "He'd heard stories about poor engineers, I guess. Anyway, Allison was there helping with the reception, and I was smitten—like, right then. It took a few months to get her to go out with me. She said her father wanted her to marry someone in his business, but I finally grabbed the brass ring, and we started dating."

"She's a lovely woman," said Carly. "I can see guys falling over to meet her."

Beau nodded. "I'm a lucky man, and I know it." He looked at his watch again. "I really need to get going. I promised Chip that I would meet him after lunch and go over some records that he's trying to understand. He hopes my Chinese lessons with Laci Lia will help interpret them."

"You speak Chinese?" Julia's mouth dropped open.

"It can be useful when dealing with one of the six countries that have nuclear submarines."

"You're just full of surprises," said Julia.

THIRTY-TWO

Julia texted Detective Monroe that Beau had just left the cafe and was on his way to meet Chip. His reply text was brief: *Thx. We're done searching.* Julia had hoped for some detail on what they might have found.

Julia ordered fresh apple pie with ice cream that she and Carly shared as their final nod to Seattle. "It looks like we'll have to go home without knowing the rest of the story after all," said Julia. "I'm sure Detective Monroe isn't going to bother letting me know how things turned out."

"We're still outsiders no matter how involved we thought we were," said Carly. "This pie is almost as good as homemade. Yum." She licked her fork for emphasis.

Julia took care of the check and waited in the doorway for Carly to return from the ladies' room. Her phone lit up one more time with a call from Monroe. "This is Julia. Did you find something?"

He chuckled and said, "You could say that. Are you free to come over to Dr. Kennedy's office? There'll be an officer at the door to let you in."

"We'll be there in about twenty minutes. You caught me as we were about to head south on I-5 heading home."

"WHY ARE we going north on the freeway?" asked Carly. "Parkview is south from here, or have you forgotten where you live?"

Julia turned and smiled. "Surprise! Monroe called while I was waiting for you and said he found something. I knew you would want to know what it was, so we're heading back to Beau's office. He said we could be there."

"Oh. Okay. Yeah, I'd like to know what your friend has been up to. I take it Monroe didn't give you any hints."

"Correct. We can let our imaginations go wild until he lays the truth on us."

Saturday traffic on the freeway between downtown and the university was light because it wasn't football season for the University of Washington Huskies, and there wasn't a home Seattle Mariners game going on. Julia pulled into the parking lot next to the engineering building, where a uniformed officer stood at the main door waiting to admit the sisters.

The building was deathly quiet on a Saturday afternoon, with no students or personnel present. Julia and Carly raced up the stairs to the nuclear engineering department office, where they found Monroe and another officer they hadn't previously met.

Monroe looked up and smiled. "Hi, Julia and Carly. Thanks for coming. This is Officer Schneider." Schneider tapped a finger salute on the brim of his cap. "We've found something we think might explain a few things. Go ahead and have a seat."

"Before I tell you what we found, let me catch you up on

some of the other details we checked out. First, one of my officers checked all the airlines for Dr. Kennedy's name. They didn't find anything in their search. I suppose he could have flown privately on someone's charter jet, but that doesn't seem likely at this point."

"Does his father-in-law have access to a plane?" asked Julia. "He seems to be quite wealthy."

"His company does have a corporate plane, but it didn't take Dr. Kennedy anywhere. We've spoken to the pilot. Dr. Kennedy and his father-in-law are not on great terms, we've been told."

"I can understand that, knowing the events of the week," said Julia as Carly nodded.

"While he likely didn't go to San Diego, it is certainly possible that he drove somewhere, perhaps to Vancouver, B.C. or to meet his friend Chip Englund at Hanford."

"I can understand him going to see Chip, but why would he go to British Columbia?" Julia furrowed her brow.

"We haven't ascertained that he went to either of those locations, but we are quite certain he didn't go to San Diego, despite his telling that tale to his wife."

"Which brings up the question of why did he lie?"

"I'm getting to that," said Monroe. He held up a manila file folder thick with documents. "We found these in Monica's desk. She's been keeping tabs on Dr. Kennedy and Dr. Englund and reporting their actions and whereabouts to Sheldon Stanley."

"Sheldon?" asked Julia.

"And Monica?" added Carly.

Monroe nodded.

"How does Laci Lia fit into this? Is she an innocent bystander?" asked Julia.

"Not so innocent," said Carly. "Remember—she had an affair with Beau. And claimed to have borne his daughter."

"Beau told us that Allison didn't know about the affair until he told her about it when their son was kidnapped," said Julia. "And that he's had a vasectomy. He already has three children, you know."

Monroe nodded. "We had a conversation with Mrs. Kennedy. She has known about the affair for at least a few months. She has kicked him out of the house several times, but they reconcile and repeat the cycle. She cites her Catholic background and the three children as her reasons for not filing for a divorce."

"There's also status in being married to a university professor," said Julia. "And Beau won't file because he's probably very attached to his father-in-law's money and status and his own reputation."

"Exactly," said Monroe.

"Does Allison know who the other party in the affair is?" asked Carly.

Monroe said grimly, "There's been more than one 'other party,' unfortunately. Ms. Ling is only the latest one."

"Men!" exclaimed Carly. "They're not very good at hiding their actions, so I don't know why they even try to get away with this kind of stuff."

"Monica was well aware of what was going on between her boss and Laci Lia, according to notes in a journal in her desk," said Monroe. "We'll be talking with her soon and learn more."

"I'd love to listen in on *that* conversation," said Carly, wiggling her eyebrows.

Monroe gave her a sidelong look. "I hope you're not serious."

Carly's face immediately went poker-face flat. "No, sir. Of course not."

Julia had been unusually quiet for a couple of minutes. "It occurs to me that someone may be doing some blackmailing. Who has the most to gain with Beau's potential breakthrough? I heard him say that the U.S. government hasn't been interested in his research. Could he be trying to sell his discovery to another country?"

Monroe leaned against the desk. "It's been done before. Sell to the highest bidder."

Julia nodded. "In this case, considering that only six countries have nuclear submarines, Beau may be flirting with the Chinese government. I say that because of his work with Laci Lia."

"Which other countries have nuclear subs?" asked Monroe.

"In addition to China and the United States, the other countries are France, United Kingdom, India and Russia." Julia continued, "France, the U.K. and India are allies of the United States, and I would think it unlikely that Beau would be working with them. China and Russia, however, are a different story."

"What would he hope to gain? It seems like he has a lot to lose if he were found out," said Monroe.

"Money is the obvious answer," said Julia. "He would be free from his wife's family money. He already has a relationship with a Chinese national and speaks some Chinese. Carly and I learned that today at lunch."

"I don't see him giving up his children," said Carly.

"He's already flirting with that every time he enters a new affair," said Monroe.

"He's slimy," said Julia, shivering involuntarily.

"We still have Lincoln Wellsmith and Chip Englund to work into the equation," said Monroe. "I suspect one of those guys is the kingpin in whatever is going on."

"Have you been able to cross-reference their email traffic to see if their paths cross in other ways? With the information you already have you should be able to request their laptops and search them," said Julia.

"Our IT specialist, Jesse, is working on that right now. He said he can duplicate their hard drives from the web and do cross-referencing that way."

"*Ooh,*" said Julia. "That's sneaky."

Monroe smiled. "That's what we get to do when we're friendly with the CIA and FBI. Their agents are gathering up our favorite suspects as we speak. I don't suppose you two ladies would like to come down to the station and listen in on the interviews?"

"Are we allowed to do that?" asked Carly.

"If I say so, yes," the detective replied.

THIRTY-THREE

Julia and Carly were ushered into a darkened room behind a one-way window, where they joined two police officers and an agent of the Federal Bureau of Investigation who identified himself as Roger Harris. Julia was well aware that their being allowed to be present was unusual, but Detective Monroe had explained that they had been instrumental in identifying certain circumstances of the investigation and were being allowed to listen as a courtesy for their help.

The police officers and the FBI agent wore serious expressions and didn't seem inclined to chitchat. The first person escorted into the interview room was Lincoln Wellsmith. Julia and Carly looked at each other with wide eyes. He hadn't been on their list as a suspect.

Detective Monroe led the questioning with Detective Snaza at his side. He asked the usual questions to verify identity, including name, address, and occupation. Lincoln seemed to have regained his memory, or most of it anyway, as signified by his ease in answering the questions. He still had a blank spot for details between the time when he was attacked from behind at the bar, which he couldn't name until he woke up in the hospital several days later.

His story jibed with what he had told Julia and Monroe in their conversations. He verified that he hadn't been in touch with Sheldon Stanley except for the emails prior to the nuclear energy conference at the Pacific Science Center the prior week. Monroe asked questions about Lincoln's work connection at Scripps and business relationships with Drs. Kennedy and Englund.

Monroe didn't question him about calling Sheldon a traitor when he had first seen that photo. Julia wondered why he held back. She turned her head toward the other officers and the agent but didn't see any evidence of a reaction from them. Lincoln was dismissed with the admonishment that he might be recalled for more questioning.

Monroe and Snaza conferred for a few moments and checked their notes before inviting the next interviewee into the room. Laci Lia Ling looked tiny and scared as she was escorted by an armed police officer to a chair at the table.

Detective Snaza asked Laci Lia the same questions about name, address, and so on. She answered in a thin, whispery voice. The confidence she'd displayed at the office when Julia and Carly first met her had evaporated. Most of the early questions were about Benjamin's kidnapping. Laci Lia professed no knowledge of the incident, although her body language suggested otherwise, in Julia's opinion. At one point, Snaza stared at her for a full thirty seconds before she looked down at her hands.

When the detective asked her to describe her whereabouts on the day that Beau claimed to have flown to San Diego, she hesitated before launching into a description of going with her friend to shop for a wedding dress. She stumbled on details such as the name of the bridal shop and where they had eaten lunch. She claimed she was nervous because of the questioning. When asked specifically about when she had first met Dr. Kennedy, she first said she couldn't recall. When asked if it had been prior to her interview at the University of Washington, she replied, "No." She looked away when Snaza challenged her and said, "I already told you I didn't know him prior to the interview."

After another few minutes of questioning without any new information having been obtained, Snaza released her. He reminded her to stay in town until she was notified that she was cleared.

Julia longed for a drink of water. She asked Agent Harris for permission for Carly and her to leave the room, and headed for the closest water fountain and ladies' room, in that order.

"Does Monroe know Laci Lia was lying about knowing Beau before she came here?" Carly scrubbed her hands twice as hard as usual. The room seemed tainted by the activity that went on in police stations.

"I'm sure he does. Snaza might not, but he'll be updated, I'm sure." Julia dried her hands in the jet dryer. She wasn't convinced they dried hands as well as good old paper towels, but she had to agree that they cut down on paper waste. And felling of innocent trees.

"I'm not sure I can take much more of this interview process," said Carly. "It's much more fun and faster to watch it on television."

"Agreed. I think I know why lawyers look older than the average person after spending day after day in courtrooms." Julia glanced at the time. "I know you want to get on the road, but can you spare one more session before we leave?"

"I guess so. The traffic will be light on a Saturday evening, and there's still daylight till eight thirty or so at this time of year."

They knocked on the door of the viewing room and were allowed to reenter. Agent Harris said, "We haven't been able to find the other three men to interview. Do you know where Dr. Kennedy was going to meet Dr. Englund after he left you?"

Julia said, "No. He didn't say."

Carly said, "All he said was that Chip—Dr. Englund—wanted some help translating some Chinese."

Harris asked, "What about Mr. Stanley?"

Julia scowled. "I'm quite sure I never want to see him again. We have no information about him since the day he took us for the limo ride."

Agent Harris managed a smile before he said, "I wonder if Dr. Englund was using a code phrase of some kind. I understand he's already fluent in the Chinese language. Are you sure Dr. Kennedy didn't give you a hint? A restaurant, maybe?"

Julia shook her head. "I'm sure that he didn't. But when we were with Dr. Englund a couple of days ago, we talked about how easy it would be to use seaplanes if someone wanted to get away in a hurry without using the major airports or railways."

"That's an excellent thought." Harris left the room hurriedly and joined Monroe and Snaza in the interview room.

THIRTY-FOUR

Monroe poked his head into the viewing room. "I'm going back up to Dr. Kennedy's office and see if there's anything he left clue-wise, like a flight schedule. Or even a note."

Julia picked up her tote as she asked, "Do you really think he'd be that obvious?"

"When people get in a hurry, they often do stupid things just like that." He raised an eyebrow. "Follow me to the parking lot. We'll take my car. We can get there faster when I turn on the lights and siren."

Carly giggled. "Just like in the movies."

Saturday afternoon traffic was light—no baseball games and nothing going on at the Convention Center. Monroe pressed the accelerator and cruised up the freeway going ten to fifteen miles over the speed limit. He turned on his lights a couple of times to break up some congestion and slid into the exit ramp for the university's southern entrance.

Two other police cars were already parked at the side of the engineering building, hidden in the shadows of the trees.

Monroe assigned one of the officers to stay with the cars and led the way into the building. He produced a key that unlocked the door and moved quietly up the stairs to the second floor.

The office was dark behind the locked door, for which Monroe had a second key. They walked through the hallway to Laci Lia's office. "Officer Hughes, you're looking for anything that might mention travel plans, *Sealab*, or the names of any of our suspects.

"Julia and Carly, come with me. We're going to search Dr. Kennedy's desk again. This time our target is anything that looks like a schedule or travel arrangements."

Fifteen minutes passed quietly except for the occasional cough or sneeze, which sounded abnormally loud in the silence.

Monroe's phone rang. "Yes. What do you have?" He nodded. "Thanks. After the secretary enters the building, arrest Dr. Englund and keep him company. I'll take care of things here.

"That was Officer Chen. Dr. Englund and Dr. Kennedy's secretary, Monica, just arrived. She's entering the building. We'll all stay here in the professor's office, Officer Johnson included, while she retrieves whatever she came for."

Julia barely breathed behind the closed door in Beau's office. She was surprised at how quickly the temperature of the room warmed up with four adult bodies inside. She heard the door open from the hallway, then the click of the light switch, and finally the squeak of a drawer that needed a big squirt of WD-40. Monroe looked at Officer Johnson and nodded his head toward the door. Johnson stepped forward and opened it quietly, startling Monica, who dropped a large manila envelope onto the floor.

"Who are you?" Monica asked, stooping to pick up the envelope.

Monroe stepped out of Beau's office and joined Johnson. "I'll take those," he said with an outstretched hand.

OUTSIDE THE BUILDING, Monica and Chip were taken away in separate police cars. Monroe had been talking on his phone for several minutes when he finally pocketed it and smiled. "It seems your friend Dr. Kennedy was planning to leave the city, but his travel plans have been modified."

"I don't understand," said Julia.

"I'll explain on the way to Boeing Field," he replied.

The drive from the university to Boeing Field normally took about fifteen minutes, but with sirens and lights, Monroe got them to the airfield in about ten.

"It seems that Mrs. Kennedy's father's company leases a corporate jet that is housed at King County International Airport, which I'm sure you know as Boeing Field. Dr. Kennedy showed up at the airport and asked to fly to San Diego. The pilot was ready to comply, but we had already talked to Mrs. Kennedy's father because she had told us about the company jet. We had him run interference in case Beau tried to use the plane."

"And here I was thinking of little seaplanes," said Julia.

"That's what made me think of corporate jets," said Monroe. "I wasn't sure if Dr. Kennedy had access to one until I talked to his wife earlier this morning and found out that he did. So your comment is what led us to check it out."

Julia glowed. "You're giving me too much credit."

Carly said, "Hey, we're here. And we're driving on the tarmac. That *is* just like in the movies." She stared at the plane as they moved in closer. Two other police cars were already waiting, lights flashing.

"The suspects are already in custody," said Monroe. "You can get out of the car if you like."

Julia and Carly piled out of the detective's car and followed him to the plane. They waited with one of the officers from the first police car while Monroe and a second officer walked up the stairs to the plane's door.

Several minutes later, Julia's mouth dropped open when she saw Laci Lia emerge from the doorway with the policeman gripping her arm, followed by Beau and Monroe.

Carly whispered loudly, "I think I see handcuffs."

Julia nodded with a grim smile. "I don't think this was part of Beau's plan."

THIRTY-FIVE

etective Monroe, Detective Snaza, Julia and Carly sat in a small conference room at the downtown Police Department.

"As you might imagine," Monroe began, "none of our 'friends' want to talk with us. They all want attorneys, but we'll see if they really want to have to wait until Monday to talk. I hope they enjoy the comforts of our jail, which was last updated in about 1995." He chuckled. "In the meantime, I thought the four of us might be able to figure out what's really been going on. I don't think it's as simple as it might appear."

They took places around the table, which was just large enough for the foursome. A pitcher of ice water and four clean glasses on a utilitarian tray held court in the middle. Monroe poured water while the others settled in.

"Julia, tell me what your thoughts are at this point, knowing what we do." Monroe took the last of the four chairs.

"I believe there is a deeper level of subterfuge going on," said Julia. "I'm convinced that there's something behind the references to China and *Sealab* beyond the emails' apparent origins. I don't think it's a reference to the old experiments."

"I'm listening," said Monroe.

"Several times, I've heard a reference to Laci Lia's background—that she has an uncle high up in the Chinese military, specifically with their submarines. We know China has nuclear submarines, but do we know how many? They could absolutely be building a bigger fleet of them that we wouldn't know about."

"Remember that Lincoln called Sheldon a traitor," said Carly. "And he was speaking Chinese at the time."

Julia nodded. "Sheldon could be the link or one of several connections to a Chinese plot. Speaking of Lincoln, have you talked with him lately? He told us earlier today that he was laying low because he's afraid of Sheldon. He also believes the emails that purportedly come from *Sealab* were meant to warn Beau, but I'm not sure of what. He asked me to relay that bit of information to you."

Monroe shifted position in the uncomfortable chair. "We haven't entirely cleared Lincoln from our list of potential bad boys, although I haven't figured out what he would be guilty of."

"How would Dr. Englund benefit from cooperating with the Chinese military," asked Carly, "if that's what he was doing?"

"I would guess it's all about money," said Julia. "Chip doesn't seem to be very well off financially and is probably near retirement age." She shrugged. "And he's probably as high on the pay scale as he's going to get. I also heard Beau say he'd had a tough, expensive divorce not that long ago."

"Go on," said Monroe.

"If Chip or Beau were able to supply the Chinese with the

information that would allow them to build new *Sealabs* or submarine stations, I bet a lot of money would change hands."

"Chip said Beau was on the brink of a breakthrough in his research lab," said Carly. "Could that be what Chip is trying to get his hands on so he can sell it to the Chinese?"

"Let me get Commander Manning on the phone," said Monroe. "He may be able to provide additional information that supports that idea."

It didn't take long for the department's information technology support person to set up the call with the base commander. He saluted as he left. Julia thought she saw him wink at Carly as he exited. When she glanced at her sister, she detected a hint of pink in her cheeks.

"The officials running the Chinese military have been said to be notoriously corrupt and don't play well with their government," said Commander Manning, speaking to the group via the newly connected speakerphone. "We've had concerns for some time that the Chinese Navy has been secretly building up their fleet of nuclear submarines, although we haven't been able to determine where they are based."

Julia raised her hand. "May I ask a question?"

Manning replied, "Go ahead. Peter, this is Dr. Julia Fairchild. I believe you met her with Dr. Englund earlier in the week."

"Thank you. Do you think the submarines would simply stay underwater instead of surfacing to a base like the one at Bangor?"

"It's certainly possible, but this whole *Sealab* idea has me thinking in a different direction. We know, or at least we believe, that China has its eyes on world domination. Imagine the possibilities if they were able to build these underwater bases anywhere they wanted, even far away from their own coastline, and use them to send their submarines to more remote posts."

"That's scary," said Julia.

"It's scarier if you visualize them with nuclear warheads pointing at Russia or the United States."

"Are you saying they could just pop up somewhere, and we wouldn't know it?" Julia shuddered as she considered the possibility.

"Our underwater detection systems have some inadequacies, although scientists are hard at work developing new technology that will expand our capabilities tremendously."

"I'm a science fiction buff," said Officer Snaza. "I can believe that the scenario you've described is absolutely possible."

"If the United States and Russia are vulnerable," said Julia, "imagine the angst of the leaders of smaller countries like Norway or Japan. Who's going to protect them?"

The room was quiet for a few minutes. Julia finally asked the commander, "We were told you gave Dr. Englund some false information when you met earlier this week. Does that have something to do with all this?"

"I may have suggested something that would cause him to take action if he were indeed planning to relay sensitive information. But that's all I can say. Detective Monroe will be managing any further intervention."

"Commander Manning," said Monroe, "thank you for your time and for being so candid with us. Please let me know if there's anything I can do to help you."

Snaza stepped out of the room to take a call. When he returned a couple of minutes later, he told Monroe that Laci Lia had decided to talk without an attorney present.

"Tell the desk sergeant to put her in an interview room,

and I'll be there in ten," said Monroe. "And bring in Lincoln Wellsmith again. I have a few more questions for him."

THIRTY-SIX

Laci Lia sat tall in the straight-backed chair in the interview room. Julia had expected her to appear small and afraid again. Her physical stature was small, as is typical for the Asian population, but she looked anything but afraid. Detective Monroe entered the room and sat on the edge of the table. After introducing himself and verifying that she did, indeed, wish to continue the conversation without an attorney present, he asked her to tell him more about herself and why she was taking the jet with Beau.

She calmly explained that she had been under pressure from Dr. Englund to share the results of Dr. Kennedy's research related to the underwater project called *Sealab*. She had refused, however, even though he had offered her fifty thousand dollars at first and increased the amount he was willing to pay every time he contacted her. It was up to a million dollars as of about a month ago.

"Where do you think he would get this kind of money?" Monroe folded his hands in his lap.

"I'm not sure, but I suspect he was planning to sell the information," said Laci Lia. She looked straight at Monroe.

"Who would be willing to pay for it?"

Laci Lia hooked an eyebrow. "I'm sure you have learned by now that I have an uncle in the Chinese Naval branch of their military. I know he would do such a thing."

"Hmm. Has he asked you to obtain this valuable information for him?"

Laci Lia nodded. "He's hinted through conversations with my father, but I would never sell out to him or the government." Her voice took on an angry tone.

"Do you know if your uncle has made any direct connection to Dr. Englund?"

"Perhaps. But I didn't help him get in touch with my uncle." Laci Lia's shoulders slumped a tiny bit for a moment, then stiffened again. "There are other ways to make such contacts."

"Okay. There's another student, Chase McGill, working with you and Dr. Kennedy. Do you know if he's been contacted by Dr. Englund?"

Laci Lia furrowed her brow. "Chase? I'm not sure. We've never talked about it. I suppose it's a possibility. He seems like a straight arrow to me, but it could be an act. Students, even senior graduate students, don't make a lot of money, and a million dollars could be tempting."

"Why weren't you tempted?"

"I come from a very wealthy family and have never wanted for anything. My father was able to escape the clutches of the Chinese government many years ago and no longer lives on the mainland. It is my uncle who clings to the empty promises of the current regime." She scoffed.

"Where does your family live?"

"In Taiwan, which is technically still part of China, but the people are more independent. My father would move to a neutral country if it became necessary to preserve his independence."

"One more question for you, Ms. Ling," said Monroe. "Where were you and Dr. Kennedy planning to go today?"

"Beau—Dr. Kennedy—said we were going to fly to San Diego to collect some recent data from the Oceanography Institute. He has an appointment on the teaching staff there."

"Yes, I'm aware of that. And then what?"

"I'm not sure what you mean."

"The pilot had filed a flight plan to go on to Mexico." Monroe looked straight at Laci Lia. "Why would you be going there?"

Laci Lia's face blanched. "You'd better talk to Beau about that. I only knew about going to the research center."

"You're sure about that?" Monroe stood and moved in closer. "Or were you two planning to leave the country?"

Laci Lia stiffened. "We were just going to San Diego."

OFFICER SNAZA, Julia, and Carly returned to Monroe's small conference room.

"She's not the weak link, I'm sure," said Monroe. He arched an eyebrow as he pulled his cell phone from his jacket pocket and read a message. "Looks like Lincoln Wellsmith is here." He pocketed the phone and reached for the door. "Detective Snaza, I'd like you to interview with me. Maybe we'll learn something new because you're a new face to him. Julia and Carly, I'll escort you to the viewing room to watch and listen."

Unlike his demeanor in the previous interviews when he seemed suspicious and antsy, Lincoln now appeared confident and comfortable despite being in a room designed intentionally to be intimidating. He was not handcuffed and sat with his legs crossed, leaning back in the metal chair.

"Detective Monroe," Lincoln said. "A pleasure to see you again."

"This is Detective Snaza," said Monroe. "Snaza, meet Lincoln Wellsmith. He's the 'John Doe' who started this whole mess."

MONROE GAVE a Cliff's note version of how Lincoln had been found by Julia and Carly at the arboretum with a head injury, followed by several days of amnesia. Lincoln picked up the narrative from the point where he had been released from the hospital in the care of his sister. He explained that he had known Sheldon Stanley from previous interactions and wasn't sure he could be trusted after the encounter downtown. He retold the story of jumping from the car and hiding in a bar until he thought he was safe, with the head injury apparently happening after showing up at the tavern.

He hadn't known Julia prior to their finding him, but he remembered her face from seeing her as they waited for a taxi and sensed that he could trust her after seeing her again at the hospital several days later. He confirmed that he had confided in her and given her some details because of that brief but memorable encounter.

"What about Dr. Kennedy? We've gotten mixed answers as to whether you two knew each other prior to this week." Monroe was sitting on the corner of the table while Snaza stood off to the side.

"Oh, we knew each other all right," Lincoln smirked. "He and I both worked at the Scripps Institution of Oceanography, although not as direct partners. He had done some graduate work in the research lab some fifteen years back before he ended up here in Seattle."

"Was there a problem between you two?" This was Snaza, who was quickly catching up on the nuances of the case.

Lincoln looked Snaza in the eyes. "Would you like it if someone tried to steal your work and claim it as your own?"

"Is that what happened?" asked Monroe.

"I'm not one hundred percent certain, but every time Dr. Kennedy came down to Scripps, it seems he was intent on learning what I might have uncovered in my own research that he could apply to his work. I didn't trust him."

Monroe paced the room for a moment. "Dr. Fairchild said you told her that Dr. Kennedy was loyal to the United States, and you didn't think he would sell out to a foreign country with this *Sealab* research project. Is that true?"

Lincoln put an elbow on the table and fingers on his chin. "I used to believe that, but recently I'm not sure."

"Why do you think that?"

Lincoln smiled. "Dr. Kennedy—Beau—is married to a lovely woman with a father who is worth millions. He and Allison have had a few rocky moments over the years. She's caught him having an affair or two and threatens to leave him, taking the children with her, of course. To this point, she's always taken him back, but there's always a possibility she won't in the future. In the meantime, he's become accustomed to a lifestyle that he wouldn't be able to maintain on his professor's salary."

"Do you think he's looking for big money by selling his research to a major buyer, like China?" asked Monroe.

Lincoln nodded and smiled. "Perhaps. But he knows that Ms. Ling's father is worth even more than Allison's father. Maybe Beau thinks he's hit the big jackpot this time and can afford to get a divorce and keep his lifestyle. And if his research project is as good as he implies, he might be able to sell out to the highest bidder as well."

Monroe looked at Snaza. "Sounds like double-dipping to me."

In the observation room, Julia whispered to Carly. "Beau seems to have forgotten that any findings from his research in either lab would belong to the university or Scripps, depending on how his contract is set up. He wouldn't be able to sell it as his own property."

"If Laci Lia really has a mega-wealthy father, he might not care," said Carly.

THIRTY-SEVEN

Lincoln was finally excused. Julia observed that Monroe was trying to find a way to connect him to any suspicious activity, but it seemed to her that he was unsuccessful, at least on the surface. Snaza opened the door to their observation room and invited Julia and Carly to join him and Monroe in the conference room again. Julia looked at her watch. She wondered if Carly was about to commit mutiny because of being behind schedule in getting home.

"I don't think there's anything we can pin on Mr. Wellsmith," said Monroe, addressing Julia. "What do you and Carly think?"

Julia was taken aback by his asking her the direct question. "I've never seriously thought he was guilty of anything, although I still don't understand that look of panic when we first saw him."

"He said he wasn't sure he could trust Sheldon. I should have asked him another clarifying question or two, I suppose, in case there was more to it than that."

Snaza opened his mouth to speak, but a knock on the door interrupted whatever he had been planning to say.

The desk sergeant poked his head into the room. "There's a CIA agent here to see you, Detective Monroe."

"Send him in," said Monroe.

The sergeant looked at Julia and Carly with a furrowed brow. "What about them?" He pointed at the sisters.

"They can stay. They know what's going on." Monroe gave a reassuring nod.

Sheldon Stanley stepped into the room, thanking the sergeant as the door closed behind him. He did a double-take when he saw Julia, then Carly, at the table with the two detectives. He recovered quickly and smiled at them. Julia's and Carly's mouths dropped open.

Snaza grabbed an empty chair that had been sitting in the corner for the agent.

"This is detective Snaza," said Monroe as Sheldon sat down and put a briefcase on the table.

Sheldon turned to his left and shook hands with Snaza. "Pleased to meet you."

"I believe you've met Dr. Julia Fairchild and Carly Pedersen earlier this week," said Monroe.

"You're a CIA agent?" asked Julia.

He replied, "I'm guilty as charged." He winked. "Sorry I couldn't tell you earlier. I hope you've forgiven me for that little car ride. It was the only way I could approach you without raising suspicion from potential observers."

"What potential observers?" demanded Julia, her own suspicion on alert.

"I can't name them for you right now, but you and your sister have been followed ever since your meeting with Beau."

"Why would someone be following us?" Julia sat up straighter.

"Probably for the same reason I decided to intervene myself," said Sheldon. "I needed to know what you might have learned from Dr. Kennedy and Dr. Englund. I had hoped you could fill in a couple of blanks related to this research project."

"Am I allowed to know why the CIA is involved in this?" asked Julia.

Sheldon looked at Monroe with a raised eyebrow. Monroe nodded his approval to let him answer her question.

Sheldon sat back in his chair and took a big breath. "The State Department had been alerted several months back about increased chatter in some channels that suggested someone was trying to sell sensitive information to the Chinese government. The *Sealab* projects of the 1960s were mentioned several times. The State Department alerted the Commander of the United States Navy Nuclear Submarine Division. For the last few months, they've been actively involved in tracing the chatter, and they finally discovered a link to Dr. Englund. That's when they called the CIA and asked us to investigate him and his known contacts."

"So, we became part of the investigation because of Dr. Englund?" Julia's eyes widened. Carly sat with her arms crossed.

Sheldon nodded. "Yes, but it was an indirect connection through Dr. Kennedy that brought you to our attention."

"I knew he couldn't be trusted," said Carly. "I warned you, Julia." She sat with one leg crossed over the other, leaning back in the chair.

"Why do you say that, Ms. Pedersen?" asked Sheldon. "Did he say or do anything in particular?"

Carly sat forward, feet on the floor. "When we went to meet him at his office, he looked pretty cozy with his grad student, Laci Lia. And he wasn't wearing his wedding ring. I know he had one on his finger when we had drinks with him the evening before. It caught my attention and made me wonder if he was having an affair with her."

Sheldon glanced at his own left hand. "Do you always notice things like that?"

Carly shook her head. "No. It's just that I had checked his left hand the evening before when I thought he was flirting with Julia."

Julia sniffed. "Sometimes she thinks she's my bodyguard."

Carly gave her sister a look. And leaned back in her chair again. "The way he was talking reminded me of the way some of the salesmen try to sweet-talk me at my office. I don't think Julia has to deal with guys like that in her medical office."

Julia said, "That's true. My office manager or the front desk staff runs interference for me." She leaned over and one-arm hugged her sister. "Back to my question of why you were tailing us. And why not tell us in the limo? We were scared to death."

"Frankly, I would have told you, except I wasn't certain that both of my colleagues were still trustworthy. We've had some leaks that we can't pinpoint, so I trust only myself and only when I'm working alone."

"Okay," said Julia. "I'll accept that as an apology, even though it seems we were being used. Were you able to learn anything that advanced your cause?"

"No, but I decided that you two were innocent bystanders in this whole mess and could probably take care of yourselves."

Monroe snickered quietly. "But watch out for the other guy if he tries to tangle with them."

Julia suppressed her desire to say something snarky and instead asked, "Have you looked into Laci Lia's background? I understand from the interview that her father is very wealthy, although she didn't say how he made his money."

"Her father is a major figure in the Chinese Communist

Party," said Sheldon. "We don't know if Laci Lia is aware that he held onto his earlier ties when he moved his family to Taiwan. And he's been in communication with Dr. Englund."

"She seems to think it's only her uncle who is still involved with the Communists," said Julia. "At least that's the impression I got when she told the police about her family." She looked at Carly, who nodded.

"He preaches anti-Communism to the public, but our agents in Taiwan have identified him as a kingpin in the Communist regime. They've learned that he stays in touch with his brother on the mainland. We believe he has a hand in the Chinese nuclear submarine program, which is obviously of great concern to us if Ms. Ling is supplying information to him or even to Dr. Englund."

Julia shivered involuntarily. "I totally get it now. She could be in danger if she returned to Taiwan, still believing in her father, but he could force her to divulge sensitive information because she wouldn't cooperate by selling it to Dr. Englund."

"She might have said some things already in candid conversation about Dr. Kennedy's research when Dr. Englund has been around," said Carly.

"True," said Sheldon. "It appears that Dr. Englund has been sending occasional messages, which could be exactly what you described."

Monroe stood up to stretch. "We've been in here for hours, Sheldon. I'm going to let these young ladies go, and let's all take a break."

CHAPTER

THIRTY-EIGHT

Julia and Carly, Monroe, Snaza and Sheldon stepped out of the conference room into a small waiting area with late afternoon sunlight streaming in through the window. Julia felt like she did when exiting the movie theatre after an afternoon show. It always seemed strange to step into the light after two hours in darkness.

Monroe said, "You're welcome to stay and listen to another interview, but you two may want to get out of here. You've been a great help. I think we can get this wrapped up with what we know now."

"Carly," said Julia. "I know you want to get home to Rob before he forbids you from traveling with me again. What about taking the train? I checked the schedule, and you can get on the 6:10 p.m. train and be in Parkview at 8:26. Will that work? I'll buy the ticket."

"Yeah, I'd like that. I'm ready to let these guys do the rest of the thinking."

Monroe said, "I can have one of my officers take you to the station if that would help."

Carly smiled and said, "I'll accept that offer. My suitcase is in Julia's car outside."

Julia hugged her sister. "I'll take care of the ticket for you."

JULIA AND MONROE WERE ALONE. He ushered her into his conference room. "Who is left for you to interview?" Julia asked him. "Didn't the others ask for attorneys?"

Monroe grinned and produced a letter-sized manila envelope from under a stack of file folders sitting on the table. "I thought you might want to be with me while I look at the contents of that envelope we took from Monica at Dr. Kennedy's office."

"Is that legal?" Julia flashed back to helping her own nephew, a deputy sheriff in her hometown of Parkview. She had been barred from knowing details several times during the evolution of that case, although she ultimately had been thanked for her help in solving the murder.

"I can defend my decision to include you in the discovery of the contents." He opened the tab closure and dumped out a sheaf of papers. "Well, well, well." He smiled at Julia. "Monica has been doing some research of her own."

"What kind of research?" asked Julia. She held out her hand as Monroe handed several sheets of printouts to her. She scrutinized the pages, which were copies of letters and documents addressed to Dr. Kennedy.

"This doesn't look like what I expected when you said research," said Julia. "These look like memos and correspondence."

Julia quickly riffled through the second set of documents that had been handed to her by Monroe. "These are definitely some of the results of the *Sealab* research that he's been doing at Scripps. They're all stamped 'confidential,' so I suspect they shouldn't have been printed or copied."

"It looks like Dr. Englund found a way of getting around Ms. Ling's refusal to work with him," said Monroe, looking over the top of his reading glasses. "I guess the department secretary needed the money more than the student."

Julia handed the documents to the detective, who returned them to the envelope. He then placed the whole shebang in a plastic evidence bag, which he sealed and labeled.

"I can believe that Monica was willing to make these copies, basically stealing Dr. Kennedy's proprietary property for money," said Julia. "But I doubt she has the wherewithal to create those fictitious emails from *Sealab* or do anything more complicated than getting into computer files using someone's password. We're missing something."

Julia sat forward in her chair, elbows on the table, chin resting on her hands. "There has to be someone else with the intelligence and greed to set this up. They would have had to be working with Dr. Englund as well since he seems to be the central person."

Julia sat up straight. "What about one of the other grad students? Chase McGill would have just as much access as Laci Lia and has been almost invisible around here. He probably doesn't have a rich daddy and might be tempted to take a shortcut to wealth after what he's seen with his fellow student and Dr. Kennedy's wife."

"Were there any other students doing research in the department?"

"I did meet another guy, but I don't recall his name. Beau said he was the newest student in the department and was working with a different professor." Julia put her arms on the table. "I would take a look at Chase."

Monroe nodded. "I like that idea. Let's find him."

. . .

A LENGTHY PHONE CALL ENSUED. It took several minutes for Monroe to firmly persuade the university telephone operator to share the address on file for the elusive graduate student, Chase McGill. Monroe made a second call to Sheldon, who agreed to meet the police officers and Detective Monroe at the residence on Shelby Street.

As was typical even when Julia had been in college, many graduate students chose to live near the university, often in houses that had been converted into apartments. Chase lived in a four-plex which had clearly once been a stately, two-story, Craftsman-style home on the south side of the Montlake cut between Lake Union and Lake Washington.

No one answered the sharp knock on the door of his apartment on the first floor, nor was there a response to the police officer telling Chase to open the door. A slight, bearded young man in tattered jeans and flip-flops emerged from the neighboring unit and informed the officer that Chase had just left. "I don't expect him back anytime soon. He asked me to take care of his cat. Gave me the food and everything."

"When did he leave?" asked Monroe, showing his badge.

"Maybe an hour ago," said the neighbor. "What's going on? Why are you looking for him?"

"Do you know where he went?"

"He said he was going to the airport. That something had just come up."

"Did he leave a key for his apartment with you, by any chance?" asked Monroe.

"I'll get it." The neighbor slipped back into his own unit.

As Sheldon listened in, Monroe took the opportunity to call the airport and request that Chase be detained.

Key in hand, Monroe and Sheldon entered Chase's apartment. The decor was a mishmash of older furniture likely inherited from earlier inhabitants of the unit. He looked around quickly before asking the neighbor if Chase had taken a laptop with him.

"I didn't see one. I'm not sure he uses one other than the one he said belongs to the university. He always uses his desktop computer here." He pointed to a battered desk in the corner upon which sat a sophisticated computer and monitor system.

"Thanks for your help." Monroe excused the young man and sat at the desk. He pressed a few buttons, and the screen lit up. Perhaps because he had been in a hurry, Chase had left his computer open to his flight plan—Seatac to Beijing. Monroe printed it for Sheldon to relay the information to TSA.

"China, huh?" Sheldon said as he glanced at the printout. "I'll gladly make the call."

Monroe nodded. "Let's see what else he has here." He scrolled through Chase's recent history and found a file labeled "Beau's research." He opened it and saw many pages of data with a summary page of conclusions. "Look at this, Sheldon. I would put money on Chase having downloaded this to a thumb drive that he's planning to sell to Laci Lia's uncle, or maybe even her father."

"I've alerted TSA in the international terminal. They'll detain him and let us pick him up for questioning."

CHAPTER
THIRTY-NINE

The following Saturday, after finishing morning rounds at the hospital, Julia drove the fifteen miles to her sister's home in the country. Carly lived on the hillside property where their Finnish great-grandparents had raised strawberries in the 1930s. At the time, there were about forty other Finnish families who each farmed twenty to forty acres of berries. Their dad had told them how the Finns had formed the Cloverdale Cooperative Berry Association and run their own processing plant near the river. The Kalama Strawberry Festival, held from 1939 to 1951 with breaks for the world war and the 1948 Vanport Flood near Portland, Oregon, boasted the world's largest strawberry shortcake. A strawberry blight, along with changing demographics, ended the era in the 1950s.

Nowadays, there isn't a strawberry field to be found in the country neighborhood unless one counted the small backyard gardens of the locals. There were several large, successful strawberry farms within fifteen to twenty miles, however, proving that the climate still supported growing the luscious berries. Julia and her siblings had grown up picking those berries in the commercial fields, earning spending money for school clothes and such. In a way, she longed for the days when kids could pick beans and berries as she had, but nowadays, the growers relied on seasonal pickers and migrants.

Julia and Carly sat on the small deck overlooking Carly's koi pond as the sun's early afternoon rays shone on their faces. Carly had fixed a small pitcher of margaritas and prepared a tray of chips and mango salsa. They relaxed in the Adirondack chairs and gazed at the Oregon hillside on the western side across the Columbia River while they watched the ships move north and south with their loads of containers filled with all kinds of goods and supplies, or cars, trucks or wheat headed to Asia. The major rivers were a significant part of the overall supply chain system, which had been sorely disrupted during the recent pandemic and now was slowly recovering.

"I'm dying to know the rest of the story," said Carly. "You told me that Chase appeared to be the blackmailer after all when we talked earlier in the week, but what else did you find out? You promised to tell me everything when you called earlier."

"Well, Beau called last evening and filled in some of the gaps for me."

"Is Beau in trouble with the law at this point?" asked Carly.

"He says that he's not being charged with anything except stupidity on his part, but Chip Englund and Chase McGill are in major trouble. And maybe Monica, too."

"Tell me the rest of the story about Chase."

"Okay. Monroe and Sheldon and I were sitting in that conference room tossing ideas around, trying to make sense of the situation. Then Monroe opened the manila envelope that Monica had tried to remove from Beau's office."

"Was it research stuff as we suspected?" Carly refilled their glasses with fresh ice and margaritas.

"Yes. So then we started talking about someone having the wherewithal to do something with that information. Chip just didn't seem savvy enough, and Monica certainly didn't have the skills necessary. The fake emails from *Sealab* were another mystery. From the sound of it, Chip could barely manage the basics of email, let alone create a fake origin."

Carly nodded. "So you thought of Chase, who would have grown up with computers and probably plays those complicated video games and would almost certainly have the skills to do everything you just mentioned. And had access. I mean, don't grad students practically live at the school?"

"Bingo. Exactly. Monroe, Sheldon and I went over to his apartment and found all the evidence they needed on his desktop. He hadn't even bothered to shut it down before he took off. He was in a big hurry to catch a plane, I guess. Anyway, the TSA officers detained him, and Sheldon retrieved the thumb drive from Chase's carry-on bag. He had downloaded Beau's files on the *Sealab* research, and we can surmise that he was planning to sell it for a tidy sum."

"That's a sad way to end a promising career. I guess trying to leave on a jet plane didn't work for him like it does in that old song."

"Beau said that both Chase and Chip are being charged with an attempt to sell sensitive material to a foreign government. He wasn't sure what would happen to Monica, although she certainly won't be working for him any longer."

Julia and Carly sat silently for a moment before Carly asked, "What about Beau and Allison? Did she finally get the courage to ask for a divorce?"

"Last night, Beau explained why he and Laci Lia were headed to San Diego. He swore he was going to leave her there to do some work for him on his research project and fly alone to Mexico. He said he needed some time and space to think about his marriage and children."

"I'll bet he does."

Julia smiled. "Allison called me a few days ago and said she and Beau had a long talk. She thanked you and me for helping the police figure out the whole story, by the way." The sisters saluted with their glasses. "And they're going to go to couples counseling. They both want to do the right thing by their children. But Beau knows this is the last time he's going to get a warning. Next time he tries to have an affair, she said, it'll be 'game over.'"

"I would think he's learned a lesson, finally. He's got a lot to lose." She shook her head. "Speaking of men, did you hear back from Josh? I figured he'd call to find out about the vacation in Seattle that he didn't get to enjoy."

Julia leaned her head back against the chair and closed her eyes.

"Are you ignoring my question? I know it might be a sensitive topic."

Julia turned to look at Carly. "You know, I never get tired of the view from here. I'm glad this piece of land is still in the family."

"I take that to mean you haven't heard more from Josh." Carly settled back in the high-backed chair. "I'm sorry."

Julia closed her eyes again and sighed just as her phone rang. It seemed out of place in the otherwise quiet of the countryside afternoon. She looked at it and smiled at Carly. "It's Josh. Right on cue." She answered. "Hi, Josh."

"Hi, Beautiful. I just got back to D.C. after spending two long, tiring weeks in New York City getting our new office set up there. What'd I miss while you were in Seattle without me?"

Julia winked at her sister as she said, "I'm not sure you'd

really want to know. The good news is I didn't find any dead bodies this time."

THE END

Acknowledgments

Thank you to my friends and family who inspire me.

A special thanks to my friend and fellow story idea conspirator, Angela Thompson. It surprises me to realize we have such devious minds when it's time to weave the final tale from the bunny trails I've created.

And ongoing love and thanks to my favorite baby sister who plays the part of Carly. Everything that happens in my stories is probably half her fault!

About the Author

PJ Peterson is an emerging author of cozy mysteries that lean to the classic whodunit style. This is PJ's sixth book in the Julia Fairchild Mystery series.

She enjoys creating mysteries that have a basis in real life and are more believable than not. With her background in internal medicine, she can't help but sprinkle a touch of medical intrigue in most of them.

Author's Note

Thank you for reading *Played in Seattle.* I hope you enjoyed it. The success of a book lies partially in reviews by readers like you. You may leave a review on Amazon.com, or Goodreads, or Bookbub, or your own favorite website.

You can always reach me at pj@pjpetersonauthor.com.

Thank you,

PJ Peterson